"He's a fine-looking boy." Ann Aimsley came to stand by her daughter at the window. "He's gentle, Gail. Just the look of him—I feel a gentleness all through him. That's why—"

"Why they picked him up for robbery—and murder?" Peter Aimsley asked.

"Peter!"

The hairs stirred at the back of Gail's neck. She stared at her mother. They all knew and were supposed to keep it from "the children." Perk had caught that, too. She looked up, her face showing so much interest that Gail calmed her own expression.

"He was innocent!" Ann Aimsley protested. "Peter, we talked about that! His friends testified to his innocence. He was acquitted!"

Peter Aimsley remained silent for a moment. Then, unable to contain himself, he blurted out, "Say what you want. But if he messes with either one of my girls, back he goes."

———————

ROSA GUY has written many distinguished books for young adults, including *New Guys Around the Block*, *Ruby,* and *Edith Jackson,* all available in Laurel-Leaf editions. A founder of the Harlem Writers Guild, Rosa Guy lives in New York City.

THE DISAPPEARANCE

ROSA GUY

LAUREL-LEAF BOOKS

Published by
Bantam Doubleday Dell Books for Young Readers
a division of
Bantam Doubleday Dell Publishing Group, Inc.
1540 Broadway
New York, New York 10036

To my sister sufferer,
Louise Meriwether

The trademark Laurel-Leaf Library® is registered in the U.S.
Patent and Trademark Office.

The trademark Dell® is registered in the U.S. Patent and
Trademark Office.

ISBN: 0-440-92064-7

RL: 5.2

Reprinted by arrangement with Delacorte Press

Printed in the United States of America

One Previous Edition

January 1992

16

RAD

THE
DISAPPEARANCE

It was almost dawn when Imamu opened his eyes and lay staring through the darkness. He was fully dressed. He put his hands out to feel the sides of his cot, but they kept reaching out until they touched the edges of a bed. The room was stuffy—the familiar stuffiness, a mixture of decay and stale wine. He was not at the youth house; he was at home.

He sat up, swung his feet to the floor, and listened. He had fallen asleep waiting for his mother. Had she come in? He got up to move toward the door and stumbled, falling back on the bed. He switched on the light and saw the duffel bag he had packed with his clean clothes in this room last night. The rest of his clothes lay scattered over the untidy room, where he had left them a month earlier, before he went to the youth house. He sure wasn't leaving much behind.

He inspected the room, as though seeing it for the first time. Most of the plaster had fallen off the walls, leaving the wooden boards exposed. The window shades had been pulled from their rollers and lay crumpled on the floor. The gray morning hulked outside the windows as though dreading to enter the room. A movement caught his eye, and he turned quickly—cockroaches were scurrying to hide beneath the worn linoleum. The sheets on his bed had turned a dark gray and would remain that way until he stole more to replace them. It would be the same in his mother's room.

Leaving the bedroom, he walked through the railroad flat to his mother's room in the front. The wall switch did not work, so he made his way to the lamp on the night table near her bed, stumbling over empty wine bottles as he went. When he turned on the light, he saw the twisted disorder of the empty bed. Disappointed at not finding her there, he reached into his shirt pocket for a toothpick. He placed it between his teeth and worked it from one corner of his mouth to the other. He had not expected her, but even so, her absence shafted him with pain.

He sat on the edge of her bed, wishing her to come home. Wishing, because he wanted no part of the scenes that came with going out to find her and dragging her home. He had never been able to stop himself. When he found her drinking on the corner or on the avenue islands with her wino friends, anger took over. He would shout at her.

"Get up. Come on, get the hell on up." Then he'd drag her away. It didn't matter if she wanted to come with him or not.

What rights did he have? None. She had taken away his rights when she had not come to jail to see him. It was over a month since he had been picked up with Iggy and Muhammed at the grocery store, where Iggy had offed old man Fein. She had to have heard about it. Someone must have told her. But she hadn't shown her face. Not at the youth center, not in the court. One month! That sure had taken away his rights.

Yet he kept sifting through his mind all of the places she might be. Hard to say. Winos usually hung around the same places, except when a new member staggered into their scene. Then they could be anywhere in the city—sometimes even out of the city. The trouble between Imamu and his mother was that he tried to keep her in the neighborhood —more precisely, in the house. He kept after her, forced her to leave her buddies, forced her to get sleep. The problem with that was that he was never willing to stay home for long with her. He had to go out. And so she kept going out and he had to keep after her. Well, she had had her way. For one month she had had her way.

Imamu took the cracked toothpick from his mouth and threw it onto the floor. He went to the bathroom, took off his sneakers, searched until he found his shoe whitener, and covered up the gray sneakers with the brilliant white polish. Then he washed, using toilet paper to dry himself because the towels were stiff with dirt. He scrubbed and polished his teeth with dry toilet paper, then went into his room, put on a fresh shirt and transferred his toothpicks from the pocket of the dirty shirt to the clean one. He was ready. But for what? To search for his old lady?

He thought of Mrs. Aimsley—her clean-looking, smooth face, her gray hair, the high lift of her head. She was a great lady.

Imamu had seen Ann Aimsley the first day of his trial. He had liked her looks. She was not much bigger than his mother—a slim five three or four. She had class. That impressed folks. He was glad she had been there to impress the lawyers, the judge. When they saw folks like her sitting in on a trial and dug she was in your corner, they didn't use just any old kind of language to bring you down. Everybody showed respect. They went by the rules then. And Mrs. Aimsley had come every day. The gray hair over her young-looking, intelligent face was saying something.

And she dug him. She had found out all there was to know about him. The week before she had seen his lawyer, talked to the judge. When she came to him she had simply said, "You mother isn't here?"

"No, ma'am," he had answered.

"Do you know why?"

"She's out there," he had answered. He hadn't wanted to lie to her.

"If she doesn't come by the time the trial ends,

would you like to come home with me?" She had never doubted that he was innocent, that he would be free. That alone pushed her tops with him.

"Yes, ma'am," he had answered. Why not? If the court didn't release him in somebody's custody, they'd more than likely send him to one of the state institutions to wait out his age thing.

Still, now that he had come home, he didn't want to leave. Leave Harlem? Go to Brooklyn? Made no sense. Leave his old lady? No way. But he had to go to Brooklyn sometime, if only to make his excuses. He had told Mrs. Aimsley he'd be there at eight-thirty. He had to keep his word. He didn't want that great lady to be waiting.

Imamu went into the kitchen and looked into the refrigerator. No food. His old lady's VA checks went for drinks. She drank breakfast, drank her lunch, and drank her dinner—when he wasn't around to get the check and cash it first. He felt in his pocket for the ten dollars that Mrs. Aimsley had given him the day before. He could go out to buy food and leave it. But that would mean he was going to Brooklyn to stay. Crazy. Not with his mother out there.

On his way back to the bedroom he heard a key fumbling in the lock. He stopped and waited in the dark behind the door. It opened, and his mother —looking smaller than he had remembered her— came into the apartment. Leaving the key in the lock, she staggered toward her room. Imamu stepped into the hall to get the key and bumped into a little man about to walk into the apartment.

"Where you think you going, man?" Imamu asked.

"Who you?" The drunk peered through his blurred eyes, trying to focus on Imamu.

"The one who's gonna knock you down those steps if you don't start walking them down."

"Me? Shit. If you game, come on." The little man put up his fists as though he remembered a long time ago. He tried to dance on his wobbly legs.

Imamu filled his eyes with hatred. He wished the little man would touch him, wished and wished he'd put one finger on him. But the little man was drunk. He was no fool.

"What's happening outcha?" his mother's hoarse voice asked. She'd come out into the hall. "Oh— it's you. What the hell you want here now?"

"I live here." He looked down at her, feeling her need for him. He wanted to embrace her, pick her up, take her and lay her on her bed. Imamu was over six feet one and—some said—still growing. He had his father's height, and looked like him, some folks said. And, like his father, he wanted to care for this frail woman. Only she wanted no part of him.

"No, you ain't," she said. "No more." Fear flickered in her dim eyes. He had forgotten that she was afraid of him—had joined the neighborhood fear brigade when he had started hanging out nights. "What happen to that woman who done took you in?" she asked.

Imamu's heart leaped with pleasure. She knew!

She had heard! She cared. She had made it her business to find out. "She done put you out?"

"Naw, she let me come home—to say goodbye."

He wanted to say that he had decided to stay. Instead he turned away from the fear in her eyes. Why was she afraid? What had he ever done to her to make her afraid? Or was she afraid for her wino friend?

"You ain't have to come back for that. You done said what you got to say. Go on back where you belong."

"I figgered I belong here."

"No, you ain't. You don't belong nowhere. Ought to be glad that lady even want you . . ."

But she knew where he was going. She loved him enough for that. Yeah, she loved him, but she was too drunk to know it.

One time that was all she had for him—love. Putting him to bed, tickling his feet. Flashes of remembered happiness included his father—before Vietnam, before the missing-in-action telegram. Long before the drinking started.

His life had been good. Never like Iggy's, who used to live downstairs. Iggy never knew his father. Iggy's old lady had never tucked him into bed or tickled his feet. His old lady had run out nights, keeping Iggy locked in. When Iggy used to cry, Imamu's mother used to send Imamu downstairs on the fire escape to keep Iggy company. Iggy was two years younger.

When Iggy's mother had found out, she had

said to his mother, "You ain't got no business tending my business, whore." His mother had simply called her "an unlettered woman" and had sent Imamu downstairs just the same.

Then Iggy's mother had started locking the windows. That was how Iggy got trapped when his apartment caught fire. Imamu and his mother had fought to bend the bars at the window to get Iggy out. Iggy's mother was gone for two days, and Iggy was kept at Child Welfare. When his mother showed up and swore that she had changed, they let him go back. But everybody knew she hadn't changed. She just wanted Iggy so she could keep on getting the Welfare check.

Not so his mother. Before that drinking, she had spent those VA checks on him, dressed him, kept him looking pretty. She had loved him.

Imamu closed his eyes, remembering: Her fresh skin smell, the feel of her arms, her soft breasts.

". . . cause Lord knows nobody else want you."

Imamu closed his eyes, remembering: her fresh moment.

"Just you go and leave us be. Come on, lil Jim, pay him no rabbit-assed mind. He mess with you, I call the police."

The little man made shuffling steps toward the door. Imamu looked down on him. "Man, if I was you I'd just be glad to be lucky. In one more second, luck's gonna quit you. And I'm gonna—"

"Gonna what?" his mother cried from behind him. "Gonna what? Gonna kill him, too?"

Blood pounded at his temples. His head felt

swollen and he narrowed his eyes. The two people looked like fleas, jumping around at his heels. He wanted to crush them with his foot. But instead he walked away, ran down the stairs and out into the dawn, into the early morning.

2

Standing with her back to the window, Gail Aimsley watched Dora Belle, her godmother, shifting her bottom around on the couch to emphasize her dislike of the plastic covering. "Ann Aimsley, you crazy as hell," Dora Belle said to Gail's mother. "A sixteen-year-old boy? From the street? But what you think you can do with he?"

Ann Aimsley laughed, reaching for the pot on the coffee table. "Have another cup of coffee, Dora Belle," she said, "because if you came here this early morning thinking you could change my mind about our foster son, you have wasted time that you could have given to your precious houses." She stressed the word "our" even as she avoided the eyes of her husband, who sat staring at her from across the table. "I have never been more sure of anyone in my life."

"But what you want with an ignorant?" Dora

Belle asked. She tossed her head, and a heavy black curl flipped from one shoulder to the other. Putting her head back, she smoothed the unbroken line of brown skin from her chin down to her chest.

Gail marveled that Dora Belle's head did not snap off. It had to be a sin for her godmother to be so vain, so conscious of every move—even with those who had known her too many years to be impressed.

"Ain't you tired of troubling with good-for-nothings?" Dora Belle went on. "They ain't know nothing. Ain't want to know. It just one more mouth." She caressed an invisible strand of hair, pulling it back from her forehead over her silky head and patting it into the heavy curl. "What I say is—"

"But there's nothing to say." Ann Aimsley leveled her intelligent brown eyes at her friend. "Except, that is, to congratulate us."

"But why you ain't talk sense in she head, Peter?" Dora Belle cried in exasperation.

"Talk?" Peter Aimsley spoke at last. "What you think I been doing? Family! She thinks she's the whole family."

Gail turned away from the complaint in her father's voice—his usual reaction whenever Dora Belle came around—and stared out the window of the brownstone. Why whine? Why hadn't he just stopped her?

Not that she blamed him. Things had been so rushed. "We must act right away," her mother had said, "or else that poor boy will be taken from the youth house after the trial and be sent to one of *those* places." It hadn't been until after her mother had made all the arrangements for the Aimsleys to be a foster family that Gail—and probably her father—had paused to wonder what was wrong with the boy's going to "one of *those* places." They should have had time to talk over a decision that serious.

But in a way Gail approved of the arrangement. She was proud of her mother. It wasn't everyone's mother who went beyond housewifely duties to form a group to help around the neighborhood. Then the group had begun to sit in on cases involving children and teen-agers in the family courts of Brooklyn and Manhattan. But unlike most mothers, Gail's had to go all the way. She was compulsive.

"Peter! That's not fair! We did talk," Ann Aimsley said.

"Talk? All I'm good for around this house is work. Bring home the bread, dig?"

"Stop, Daddy," Gail cut in. "Mother did discuss it. I heard her."

"Heard her?" Peter Aimsley's bushy eyebrows met angrily. The cast in his left eye, however, made his face look like a small boy's. "What you heard your mother say was that she thought it would be nice for someone to offer this poor boy a home. You heard me answer, 'Yes, it would.' Where I come from folks don't call that a discussion."

"Where I come from neither, Peter." Dora Belle twisted her shoulders coquettishly.

"Oh, Aunt Dora, where you come from!" Gail

waved her hand in dismissal. Dora Belle and her mother had been friends for over twenty-five years —ever since Dora Belle had come to the United States from the Island and Ann Aimsley had moved to Brooklyn from Harlem. They had gone through most women's things together—first love, disappointments in men, illness, and childbirth, Gail's birth and her sister's. Yet whenever there was an argument, Dora Belle supported Gail's father. Loyalty didn't count with her—only men.

Her father jumped on Gail's words. "Yes, goddammit, where I come from." Then Gail realized why Dora Belle had come so early. Her father had gone to her for support.

"Please, Daddy, don't be crude. If you're not willing to give our own a chance, who will?" Her father stared across the room into her large brown eyes, then shifted his away. He vacillated between being proud of and encouraging her ability to argue and feeling cowed and angry when she crossed words with him.

"You!" Her godmother pointed her angry slanting eyes at Gail. "You and this black thing. Is you what put this damn stupidness in your mother head. Political prisoners and such! Militant. Stupidness. But what it is? Is we fault if society chain we boys to the street? Is we fault if they ain't got, and ain't got mind to get? We work. Hard, hard, hard. Even your mother self. Ask she if she ain't scrub floors and send sheself to school nights, long before she get chance to call sheself housewife.

"And chance? Who need chance is you. You and

Perk." She spread her arms to include Perk, who was upstairs dressing for school. "You in college. Them big words you like to throw about ain't putting you through. Is money!" She threw a sympathetic smile toward Peter Aimsley.

"And two lovely girls so. How you know what trouble you bring on they head? A ignorant street boy?"

"Stop it!" Ann Aimsley cried, her thin lips tightening. Gail wished her mother would put Dora Belle in her place, tell her that it had been her decision, that she was the militant, the one who understood the need of the young out there on the streets. Instead her mother said, "Why call trouble on ourselves? I—I—we are in this world to do for others—as well as our own."

"Ain't that sound sweet, Peter?" A smile twisted Dora Belle's full lips.

"Peter has always wanted a son," Ann Aimsley went on.

"Yeah," Peter Aimsley snorted. "A sixteen-year-old baby son."

"Gail and Perk have always wanted a brother. And Imamu needs a home."

Bravo, thought Gail. But why put it on her father, on her and Perk? Why did her mother make her greatest moment sound like an impulsive act? It was a noble cause, a great gesture. It complemented Ann Aimsley. It went with her plain, intelligent face, the dignity of her gray hair. Gail looked at her mother as she bent to pick up a minute speck from the rug and put it in an ashtray. She stared at the empty ashtray. God, didn't she deserve a son if she wanted one?

She kept a good home. A great home, free and clear of mortgage after twenty years of struggle. It had large rooms, free now of roomers except for her father's old friend Mr. Elder, who was dug in like a tick for life. The house was well kept, well kept up. The original features of the old brownstone had been preserved: the mahogany woodwork, the marble mantelpiece, the wood-burning fireplace. The hardwood floors were protected by wall-to-wall carpeting just as the furniture was protected from dirt by clear plastic covers. Reproductions of famous paintings gleamed respectfully from shining frames. The one original painting, over the couch, was unframed. The entire house had a clean feeling, a sense of conforming to the modern health standards Ann Aimsley had insisted upon long before she had gone out on her crusades. An everyday sameness prevailed, cloaking the family in a sort of perfection. All that was left for her parents, Gail thought, was to grow old—the successful couple. Didn't her mother deserve whatever she wanted? But something in Gail also asked, Why change things?

Dora Belle kept spinning off her hard-hitting words: "But if all you does want a boy so bad, how come you ain't have one, Ann?"

"Do you expect me to have a child every ten years? Not with so many children out there needing homes. After all, Gail is seventeen."

Peter Aimsley jumped to his feet and walked up

and down the room. "If he needs a home so bad, why ain't he here? Why didn't he come home with you from court yesterday? Why he had to go see his mother? From what you say, she didn't go to see him in court. What he got to go looking for her for?"

"She's still his mother, Peter."

"Yeah, but I got my shop to open. I don't get this—opening up late just because he don't make time."

"Me, too," Dora Belle said. "I got things to do. I run here this morning and leave me door open. And he yet ain't come."

"Why do you always leave your door open?" Ann Aimsley asked, glad to change the subject. "One day you'll go back and—"

"Who thiefing from me?" Dora Belle shrugged. "With all me neighbors looking? With me two houses full with people? A thief must be looking for the way to the jailhouse. And what to thief? Me furniture? Let he. It insured. Anyway, I leave it open in case me man come back when I ain't there. I want one big surprise when I find he in me bed—"

"Stop that!" Ann Aimsley spoke sharply. Dora Belle backed down.

"Ann dear, why you vex with me? I only—" She broke off as Perk came into the room. "Eh-eh," she said. "But look who here. Me precious heart."

Fully dressed, but with her uncombed hair standing out thick and heavy over her head, Perk came in. She was grinning, exposing her gums where her front teeth were missing. Running into Dora Belle's arms, she lisped. "Godmother, I want you to comb my hair."

"Eh-eh, Perky," Dora Belle exclaimed. "But ain't that the skirt I buy you? God, you grow."

Perk turned around to show off the red plaid skirt, which barely topped her chubby legs. She was a pretty child. She looked more like her parents than Gail did—Gail was the darkest in the family. Perk at eight was all golden—her hair, her complexion, her eyes.

"You going to comb my hair?" she asked again, leaning against her godmother and playing with the locket on Dora Belle's high chest.

"What?" her godmother answered. "And have your mother hand me me head in me hand when I get a piece of hair on she rug?"

"But I want to look as pretty as you."

Dora Belle was more than pretty, she was beautiful. She wore a shocking-pink dress which set off her deep brown skin. When she had come in, Peter Aimsley had remarked that she stunned the morn out of the morning. She was straight-backed, tall, and full-bodied. She looked about thirty, instead of forty-five.

"Eh-eh." Dora Belle brightened. "But you see why I love this child? She smart, smart, smart. Yes, Perk, me love. I ain't care what that woman say. I combing your hair." She pulled the locket from Perk's hand. "Leave me chain, nuh. If you break it, I putting one on your arse."

"No, for God's sake, don't break that chain." Peter Aimsley laughed. "That locket looks too good where it's at."

"Is me man what give it to me," Dora Belle said, looking at Ann Aimsley slyly.

"Who?" Perk asked. "You mean that man I saw in your house the other day?"

"Like I say, she smart like anything but she mouth too damn big," Dora Belle said. "Ain't you know how to hold your tongue?" But at Perk's contrite expression, Dora Belle pressed Perk to her chest. "Go get the comb." When Perk ran out of the room, Dora Belle said, "Is me man Jacques what give me."

"He sure got good taste." Peter Aimsley smiled.

"You make joke, Peter, but is true." She returned his smile. "Why you think I love that man? Why you think I still waiting for he? He know how to suit me." She fingered the golden locket. "Is me engagement. We going to do that forever thing when he ship come back."

"Forever?" Peter Aimsley asked. "Dora Belle, what in the world will you do with one man forever?"

It was an ongoing joke among them that Ann Aimsley needed one man and one house, while Dora Belle had always needed many men and many houses. That was why Peter Aimsley had married Ann, even though he had been seeing Dora Belle first.

"You ain't never try to figure out, so why you asking?" Dora Belle looked suggestively at Peter Aimsley.

Gail turned from them to examine the tree outside the window. Across the street at the Millers —the only other American family on the tree-lined block—she could see old Mr. Miller, fat and slow, shuffling with his empty garbage pails from the curb to his front yard. Gail stuck her head out of the window. She looked first up and then down the block.

"I wish he'd hurry and come," she said. "I want to see him before I go to school. I promised Celia I'd tell her all about him."

"He's a fine-looking boy." Ann Aimsley came to stand by her daughter at the window. "He's gentle, Gail." The pleading sound in her mother's voice made Gail feel again her mother's doubts. It unsettled her. "Just the look of him—I feel a gentleness all through him. That's why—"

"Why they picked him up for robbery—and murder?" Peter Aimsley asked.

"Peter!"

The hairs stirred at the back of Gail's neck. She stared at her mother. She turned to look at Dora Belle, who kept on combing Perk's hair. She knew! They all knew and were supposed to keep it from the "children." Perk had caught that, too. She looked up, her face showing so much interest that Gail calmed her own expression.

"He was innocent!" Ann Aimsley protested. "Peter, we talked about that! His friends testified to his innocence. He was acquitted!"

Peter Aimsley remained silent for a moment. Then, unable to contain himself, he blurted out, "Say what you want. But I ain't taking this much." He measured the tip of a hardened finger with a worn-down fingernail. "If he messes with either one of my girls, back he goes. I don't give one damn, do you hear? Not one damn about your simple-assed causes." Before Ann Aimsley could say anything, the door bell rang.

3

She could be my sister, Imamu thought of the tall, dark, slim girl who opened the door and stood studying him. He liked the intelligent look of her wide, round eyes. Her low boots, the slacks hugging her slim hips, the shirt open at the neck gave her a sporty look. But as he looked into her eyes they changed—cooled. She resented his boot-to-face inspection. Hell, he had to look her over. Right? Right. But he masked his feelings as he followed her through the foyer into the living room, where he found himself bombarded by stares, giving *him* a going-over.

Reaching into his shirt pocket, Imamu took out a toothpick, put it between his teeth, and moved it around with his lips. He lowered his eyelids to look the room over without seeming to and to put down the stares without being out-and-out evil. But then

Ann Aimsley came toward him with outstretched hands.

"Imamu, welcome."

The shock of seeing this pleasant-looking, gray-haired lady with the friendly smile in her own setting moved him to smile. He apologized. "Didn't mean to be late."

"But you did come. Welcome." He believed her. "And I suppose you're anxious to meet this family you are getting into."

Imamu raised his eyes, but his gaze skimmed across the room and he found himself looking into the eyes of the finest woman he had ever seen in his life. She sat on the couch, combing a little girl's hair, but she had managed to get his attention by a trick of her eyes. Then she gave a little laugh.

"My but he ain't a child a-tall. He a young man. A pretty young man."

"The children's godmother," Ann Aimsley said. "But please, meet your foster father, Mr. Aimsley."

Mrs. Aimsley had told him about her husband. Still, he had not expected a man in the house. Now, when he saw Peter Aimsley's muscular arms and broad shoulders, Imamu's thoughts started to tiptoe, and he was glad he hadn't given more than a once-over to the girl at the door. He wanted to get away.

But when Peter Aimsley said, "John Jones, is it?" Imamu answered sharply. "Imamu is my name."

"What kind of a name is that? Some cult name or something?"

"No, sir." Imamu kept his voice even, cool. He

didn't want to make mistakes. He didn't want the dude to make any, either. "Muslim," he said.

Actually, he had never practiced Islam or any other religion. The idea of being Muslim had appealed to him because they X'd drinking. And because he leaned that way, he had decided to X smoking, too. But the only reason he didn't eat pork was because they hadn't come up with any Kentucky Fried pork places yet.

The name Imamu, though, he dug the most. Didn't want folks messing with it. He was no John. Didn't like John. Didn't take to it any more than he had taken to his father's dying in Vietnam— just another John.

"What's wrong with John?"

Imamu hoped that Peter Aimsley wasn't going to push him into jumping back. He'd sooner leave. But Ann Aimsley hooked his arm and turned him away from her husband, toward the girl who had opened the door.

"Imamu," she said, "this is Gail. She has been waiting at that window all morning for you."

"I certainly was, Imamu." Gail held out her hand and smiled as though she had forgotten his eye-balling earlier. "Both Perk and I have been dying to meet our new brother." He appreciated her calling him by his name, but her eyes were too careful, her words too proper. Phoney. He turned from her.

"Take them hands, man," Peter Aimsley said. It was an order.

"Daddy," Gail said, "you can't force Imamu to

take my hand if he doesn't want to." She spoke like someone who always had to be on the right side of things.

"Ain't forcing nobody to do nothing, puddin'," Peter Aimsley said. "I'm just telling him to take it, that's all. When somebody give you their hands, man, just take it. That's the polite thing to do."

Imamu's nostrils flared. He had and had not seen Gail's hand. But now that the dude was ordering him to take it, he couldn't lift his own if he tried to. The cat was far out. If he didn't want him in his house, all he had to do was say so. There'd be no hurting. He'd just split. But he wasn't taking this kind of big-man stuff. No way.

Peter Aimsley didn't wait for him to respond. He walked over to him, grabbed his hand, and pumped it. "See, John, that's the way we do it."

Imamu tried to take back his hand, but the older man's grip held firm. "See," Peter Aimsley said, "being the man in this house gives me the right to make sure the inmates act right." He let Imamu's hand go with a laugh that, if it was supposed to be friendly, didn't make it. The toothpick in Imamu's mouth traveled from one side to the other and back. His eyes were drawn to the fine woman on the couch, but knowing that was not wise, he raised them to the painting over her head.

The painting was of heavy waves, which broke into a foaming mass in the center of some ocean. Small shadowy objects could be seen in the dark swirl of water under the foam. The painting was large—it reached almost to the ceiling—so Imamu took his time looking at it while Peter Aimsley kept up his big-man show. "This house is run a certain way, dig? You might as well know that from the get-go. I like the way it's run. Don't want no changes. Got me, John?"

"Finish!" Dora Belle spoke loudly from the couch. But she was talking to the little girl. "Now, Perk, love, ain't you look nice? Like a doll!"

Perk stood up, feeling the long curls which hung to her shoulders. She grinned at Imamu.

"Yes, this is our little Perk," Ann Aimsley said. She looked relieved. "She does look lovely, Dora Belle—even though a bit old-fashioned."

"Ch-ups." Dora Belle sucked her back teeth. "Who say? That's how I like to see young children look. I ain't like the way these young people does do their hair today a-tall."

"I like it," Perk agreed. "It makes me look like Godmother. Don't it—John?" She grinned again.

"Really, Dora Belle," Ann Aimsley said, "you live in yesterday's world. Haven't you heard? Today we are trying to find a link to our African heritage."

"Say what you want," Dora Belle snapped, "I ain't want this little one to cut off she hair and go pickey-headed so." She nodded at Gail's Afro.

Gail laughed, but her mother said, "Gail looks perfectly lovely with her haircut."

"Well, you is the mother." Dora Belle patted her own hair. "But if this little one cut off she hair, I cutting she backsides."

"God, you are brainwashed," Ann Aimsley said. "We are past that good-hair-nearer-to-white—"

"Eh-eh." Dora Belle cut her off rudely. "And you? You ain't brainwash? So you cut your hair, letting it go gray like some old lady. But look at your house. Proper Hansel and Gretel house. The ashtray 'fraid to receive ash. And this plastic thing" —she lifted one hip—"sticking to the arse. You want everything to stay looking so, never get old. If you ask me, is better to dye your hair and take this damn cover and throw in the garbage."

"Imamu, forgive us." Ann Aimsley seemed genüinely surprised at her friend's attack. "We really are not this way. We are not a warring family. Have you had your breakfast?"

Imamu kept his eyes on the painting. He had come to be a part of a family, share family life. But already he had had it.

Dora Belle sat on the couch below his gaze. Her beauty had already slipped in his eyes. He just didn't dig anybody, but anybody, putting down the great Ann Aimsley.

"Pay no attention to Daddy." Gail came over and kissed his cheek. "He's not always like that, Imamu. We have to get used to each other, that's all." Then, turning to her father, she said, "Daddy, if you drive me, I'll make it to school on time."

"Well, I wasted my whole morning," her father said. "A little more time can't hurt. You too, Perk."

"Can I kiss you, too?" Perk asked Imamu. Imamu kept staring at the painting. Peter Aimsley picked up his youngest daughter and held her near enough to reach out to Imamu. Imamu stepped back. The toothpick snapped in his mouth. He stared with hostility at Peter Aimsley. "Is this one of them things I got to do?"

"You ain't got to do nothing," Peter Aimsley snapped. "You ain't got to do one damn thing."

"Go, go." Dora Belle stood up. She shooed the family to the door in front of her. "Go right now. This minute. All you done start off on a bad foot, and it ain't make sense to take one more step."

Ann Aimsley went out of the room with her family, and Dora Belle came over to Imamu. She hooked his arm with hers and tried to guide him to the couch. "Never mind Peter," she said. "You hear he talk? He like to bark, but he bite like a dog what ain't got teeth. Come sit by me, nuh."

Imamu resisted, and she leaned against him, speaking softly. "But when I say I ain't like Afro, I ain't mean you. I does like the way it look on men—young men." She smiled, showing off her even teeth. "And that name Imamu . . . oh, God, but is sweet." She pulled him down to the couch just as Ann Aimsley walked in, followed by a man. The newcomer wore a black overcoat and black felt hat pulled down over his beetling brow. He looked strange, out of place, on such a warm spring day. Splotched brown skin covered his sunken cheeks and high, wide cheekbones.

"Mr. Elder, meet the newest member of our family," Ann Aimsley said. "My foster son just came home today. Imamu, Mr. Elder lives on the top floor." The man nodded to Imamu, then quickly turned to Dora Belle.

"Eh," he said to her. "But you here? I ain't see you in a time."

"But why you want to see me?" Dora Belle jumped to her feet. "Looking like a jombie ready to fly to some cave. How you want to see me?"

"But you—you look good," the man answered, his voice soft. "You always look good."

"And how I must look?" she snapped. "You got reason to give why I mustn't look good? Don't trouble your head to think. You done say enough already. I gone."

It took her only a second to pick up her handbag and brush by Mr. Elder on her way to the door. "Ann, dear, but you do yourself proud." She gave Imamu a long look. "Broadening me family base so. I want a chance to talk to he. I leaving to go fix his breakfast. Bring he."

Her abrupt manner seemed to amuse more than annoy Mr. Elder. He followed her to the door. "But how Jacques is?" he asked. Dora Belle fumbled with the knob in her haste. "When last you hear from he?"

"And what Jacques got to do with you?"

"With me? What a man like Jacques got to do with me? What I got to do with he? Nothing. He too complex. I ain't like complex people."

Dora Belle spun around, hissing, trying to waste

him with a sneer. Unmoved, Mr. Elder skinned his lips back into a smile, exposing rotten front teeth. The door slammed, hard. Mr. Elder stood staring at the closed door. Then, bowing his head, he turned and walked up the stairs, quietly melting into the dark at the top.

Imamu felt his scalp crawl. "Weird-looking dude," he muttered.

"Mr. Elder?" Ann Aimsley asked. "He's a lovely man. Believe me. A very lovely man."

Imamu's eyes shied from hers. Anybody looking like that, and bringing that kind of feeling out of a woman, lovely? But then Mrs. Aimsley had said it. It had to be.

4

"Well, he came," Gail told Celia, as they settled themselves at a table in their favorite corner of the college cafeteria. "Can you imagine? A new brother —at my age."

"What's he like?" Celia asked.

"You hardly expect me to know."

"Didn't you see him?"

"Only for a little while. He didn't come last night. He came just before I left this morning."

"So?" Celia waited, smiling. "You saw him. What does he look like?"

"He—he's tall."

Gail tried to make her voice dull, uninteresting. She knew that she wasn't being fair. Celia had been waiting for Imamu's arrival almost as anxiously as she. For the past week they had done nothing but discuss the new development. Now that he had actually come, she felt a reluctance to discuss him. Why?

"Tall?" Celia said, her eyes widening. "How tall?"

"How do I know?" Gail said; then, hearing herself, she changed her tone. "I guess he's over six feet—he's taller than I am."

"Wow! You don't mean it, Gail."

"He's only sixteen, Celia," Gail reminded her.

"So?"

"So I think it's terrible for people to make over boys—younger boys—just because they happen to be good-looking."

"Good-looking! Who made over him?"

"Aunt Dora."

"What? Dora Belle, the gorgeous?"

"She was shameful."

"That means he can't be all street, Gail."

"I don't know!"

"But you can tell." Celia was insistent. "How does he walk? How does he talk? What did he say?"

"He isn't the most open person in the world."

That's what she had expected—hoped for: an underfed, undernourished street kid, with down ways. Hadn't her mother led them to believe just that when she spoke of the poor, deprived juvenile whose mother had deserted him, left him to the mercy of the court? Their attitudes had been tuned to this. Dora Belle was ready with her indictment, her father had his stern warnings, and she was prepared with loyalty and support for him—for her mother's sake. Then in he had come, tall, slim, good-looking, with large, sleepy eyes, the look of the poet—and the feel of the street oozing out.

Gail was confused, and had been ever since she had opened the door and seen Imamu. God, her mother had really pulled one this time. Little boy? Little brother? Had she done it deliberately? Just so that Dora Belle would sit up and pull that switch? What disturbed her most was that it all had a familiar feel, as though it had happened before.

"I just hope that Mother didn't make a mistake."

"Mistake? How's that?"

"I'd hate anything to happen."

"Happen?" Celia looked at her. "But of course things will happen. We know that. We talked about it. You can't expect him to crawl into your house and grow plastic covers because you were good enough to take him in."

"I don't mean that." But Gail didn't know what she meant. Something was already happening. She felt frightened, wanting to run, to get away. She wanted to go home.

"What do you mean?" Celia asked. "After all, the only point in helping what we call political prisoners is because we accept the fact that they have been crushed by the system."

"Imamu doesn't seem like someone who has exactly been crushed—by any system." Gail sipped her milk moodily. When she and Celia had talked about the victims of the system, they had meant people whose daily needs had forced them into criminal acts—a criminal mentality. She had expected someone who might steal, stay out nights, snatch pocketbooks, someone who needed to be defended—not Imamu. "He doesn't act the way I expected," she said.

"How did you expect him to act?"

"Different."

"You mean he didn't come in saying thanks?"

"That's not what I meant at all." Gail stared angrily at her friend. "And I'd thank you not to twist my words around. God, we are not the enemy."

"I'm sure he knows that."

"I'm not sure. You ought to see how he acted to my father."

"How did your father act toward him?"

Stereotyped, out of line, she wanted to say. Instead she said, "Not nice. Not nice at all."

"When do I get to meet him?"

"He's only sixteen."

"You said that before. What has that got to do with anything?"

Gail had never thought Celia was good-looking. But now she saw more than her pimpled face and her mud-colored hair, saw her gray eyes behind her eyeglasses, and realized that with the smallest effort Celia might be a beauty. Feeling guilty, Gail turned away.

"Gail, answer me," Celia said. "Because he's sixteen, I can't meet him?"

"I didn't say that." Gail's confusion grew worse. "I just don't see why you should be interested in a boy that much younger than you. Besides, he's a high school dropout. I don't think he even went one year!"

"I don't get it." Celia gulped down the last of her milk. "I know your father, your mother, godmother, and sister. Now I have to have motives because I want to meet your new brother. And don't think I don't see through you. You just don't want to share him!"

Gail felt shame burn her face. "Stop twisting what I say!"

"I'm not twisting anything," Celia said. "You are. And I'm trying to understand why. What's with you? Overnight you changed. Can it be, Gail Aimsley, that you are one of those people who do a lot of talking, but when it comes to practice, it's another thing? You're just an ordinary *petite bourgeoise*."

"How can you say a thing like that?" Celia knew how she prided herself on being intelligent, different. How she hated to be thought ordinary. "All I said was I just met him this morning. I have to get used to him."

"And then I can meet him?" Celia's voice was sharp with sarcasm. "When you get him to act right?"

"You are in a mood today, Celia. Trying to impose all your middle-class values on me. I don't have to listen." Celia wasn't going to force her to accept blame for the argument. Gail rushed out of the cafeteria.

But she knew she had been to blame. I'm sick,

she told herself. I'm going to have my period soon. Yes, that's it.

By the time Gail let herself into the house later that afternoon, she had convinced herself. She walked up the stoop determined to go to bed, to stay out of her mother's way, out of Imamu's way. Perk could bring her some soup up to bed.

But when she opened the door, the house was silent. No cooking smells rose from the kitchen. No cheerful voice called to her. So she went down to the kitchen. The very cleanliness of the stove, the walls, the refrigerator, the unlived-in look of the much-lived-in room sharpened her disappointment.

Before going upstairs to her room, she went into the living room. She wished it was morning again and they could start off from the beginning. She would stand at the window, and when the bell rang her mother would go to the door. Then when he came in she would turn—no, it would happen again: that first impression, that first shock.

She went upstairs. The light under Perk's door made her push it open. Perk was lying across the bed, coloring in a book. "Where is everybody?" Gail asked.

"Dunno," Perk answered without looking up. "Nobody was here when I came. Mr. Elder let me in." Didn't it seem strange to Perk, this change of routine, this silence, the lack of cooking smells reaching up out of the kitchen to tempt the hungry?

"It's almost six o'clock and dinner isn't even started," Gail said, forgetting she had planned to stay in bed through dinner. When her complaint didn't get a response from Perk, she added, "I just hope that Imamu didn't get her into anything today."

"Like what?" Perk looked up, a smile lighting her eyes.

"I mean, she can't neglect us just because he's here."

The smile widened to Perk's mouth. "He sure is good-looking."

"He's Okay." Gail shrugged.

"I like him, too," Perk said.

Why "too"? Gail wanted to ask. Instead she retorted, "You don't even know him."

"He's our brother," Perk said, "so we have to like him."

It was a baited answer and Gail refused to be drawn in. "Then why were you so mean this morning?"

"I wanted to see him get mad. Did you see his face when Daddy called him John?"

"You wanted him to hit you?"

"No, I wanted to see him take off on Daddy."

"Perk!"

"He didn't." Perk shrugged.

"Doesn't it matter to you that he might have? If Imamu had hit Daddy, he wouldn't have been able to stay, you know." Once it was out, Gail had to admit it mattered that he did stay, that she was glad that Dora Belle had been there and had been able to turn a bad moment around with her knowhow.

"I didn't think about that." Perk looked contrite. Born long after hopes of another child in the house had died, Perk was precious to them all. She was spoiled, quick-tongued, irresistible. With her hair (which had been so lovely that morning) disheveled and her inquisitive eyes reflecting her always busy mind, she looked like an imp.

Gail looked around Perk's room, at the white painted furniture, the matching curtains and bedspread printed with green animals, the bookcase with its rows of neatly lined-up books. Their mother still cleaned Perk's room, although she refused to touch Gail's. An unreasoning jealousy made Gail vindictive and she said, "That was really a cheap trick. As cheap as Aunt Dora coming here to support Daddy, and running out on him at the first sight of a good-looking face."

"Don't talk that way about Godmother."

"I'll talk any way I want," Gail said, satisfied that she had rid herself of her peevishness. "Just don't let me hear you causing trouble in this house again."

"I said I didn't mean it."

"In the future think before you talk." That was like telling Perk to stop breathing. Perk talked about everything. She was good at it, having begun to talk long before she toddled.

But she promised. "I will." Her contrite air made her appear roguish, rather than repentant. She was adorable. Gail reached out to brush back the heavy, golden hair. Perk jerked her head away. "Don't. I want my hair to stay looking nice for tomorrow. We're having a Memorial Day party at school."

"I guess you haven't looked in the mirror since

you came home," Gail said, laughing. She turned to leave and came face to face with Mr. Elder, standing in the doorway. Startled, she cried out shrilly, "What do you want in here?"

"I came to ask after your mother," he answered.

He was right, of course. Organization was her mother's religion. She should have started dinner.

"You are not supposed to come to our rooms," she reminded him coldly.

"I standing outside this door, Miss Lady," he said, correcting her mildly. "And I come wondering after your mother." He disappeared as quietly as he had come.

"God, the way that man sneaks around."

"He doesn't sneak," Perk said. "How do you expect to hear someone walk up on the rug?"

"You knew very well that Daddy says . . ."

Her retort was cut short by her father's voice calling upstairs, "Anybody home?" Gail ran from Perk's room into hers, feeling silly, argumentative, cluttered up inside. She seemed to be at odds with everybody.

5

"One year already I get this house, I tell you. One year! And is now they start work on it. This week! Being a woman is hard, yes?" Dora Belle smiled over Ann Aimsley's head at Imamu as the three of them climbed over the clutter of workmen's tools, bags of plaster of Paris, and electrical wiring to get down the steps. "Me other two houses now don't give me no trouble," she said. She was talking about the one directly across the street and the one down the block in which she lived. "They bring good money. How to start this one is me cross."

"You!" She snapped at a worker who had stopped his work to stare open-mouthed at her. "I ain't paying you to look. I already got man enough to look at me. Is your hand and sweat on your blasted face I spending good money for."

The man bent over his work, but Dora Belle kept complaining. "All you does charge by the hour to stand still, mouth open. It ain't horseshit I shoveling in it. Is money."

Then she smiled at Imamu. "I tell you, Imamu, they does stretch one hour to one whole day. Why? I a woman alone."

Imamu looked down at her, wanting to smile but not daring to. Instead he played his toothpick around in his mouth while letting a sympathetic look soften his eyes.

He and Ann Aimsley had come over for lunch, and Dora Belle had been playing house since. She was dressed in a shining red housecoat, short enough to show off her shapely legs, and slippers that bared her manicured toes. Ann Aimsley had seen him looking at her, admiring her, and had said, "You'll get used to Dora Belle. She always looks like that. I have been knowing her for years and have never seen her look different."

Dora Belle had waltzed around her big kitchen as though it was a ballroom, serving them hot meat patties, codfish cakes, and fried bread. They had spent the better part of the day there. The visit to the house she was renovating had been an excuse to hold them—to hold him. This pleased Imamu. It made him feel she needed him in a way that Ann Aimsley never would.

"I certainly will be glad when your Jacques comes back, Dora Belle," Ann Aimsley said. "I'm sure you both will be happy. At least you'll have a *man* to help you."

Dora Belle ignored her. She talked to Imamu. "I tell you, the new boiler done in—it all modern and thing. Me plumbing done. How to make these worthless men finish?" She turned a switch on the way down into the cellar. Ignoring the mounds of plaster and concrete strewn around the cellar floor, she pointed with pride at a new oil burner.

"When is me who do it, it get done," she said. Then she hooked Imamu's arm and squeezed it. They went back upstairs together, trying to walk on the narrow steps that were just wide enough for one. Her thighs were pressed against his, and her strong perfume in his nostrils opened up his head. I hear you, lady, I hear you. You might, just might, have yourself a man.

Yet part of himself pulled back. Things didn't happen to him that fast. Just the day before he had been let out of the youth center. This morning he had awakened in his wreck of a room in his mother's apartment. It wasn't evening yet, and here someone was offering him—that's what it seemed—herself and three houses. Made no kind of sense. Good luck and him had been strangers too long.

He had known guys who had lucked up. Beau Charles, one of the pretty boys from around the block, had been plucked out of school and had been set up—good—by a blond actress. Beau used to come around the block in his white Cadillac, bragging. But that was *once* upon a time. For the most part dudes who made it out of the block did so by hustling—chicks or drugs.

Not that he put himself down. Being tall for his age made things happen. Ever since he was thirteen he had been propositioned by older women. He just wasn't the kind of dude who picked up on them. But then he'd never had an offer from anybody as fine as Miss Dora Belle. Man!

On their way back to the brownstone where Dora Belle lived, Ann Aimsley said, "Imamu probably will be starting school next fall, Dora Belle. I'm sure he'd love to help you, but he'll be needing a summer job to help himself out."

"But how you mean?" Dora Belle said, insulted. "I ain't giving he a chance?"

Ann Aimsley laughed. "Dora Belle, you know that you are quite mad. You'll never change. I certainly hope your Jacques hurries back.

"Imamu." Ann Aimsley turned to him. "Dora Belle has one handsome fiancé. They are going to get married as soon as he gets back. He's a merchant seaman."

"Marry?" Dora Belle said. "How you know we marrying?"

"You haven't kept it a secret," Ann Aimsley said, raising her eyebrows. "Everyone believes it."

"The man gone a year, and a woman like me, what she doing by sheself? One whole year? Imamu" —she forced him to look into her glittering black eyes—"ain't it that people is to enjoy—with the hand, the ears, the nose? Absence, that like dreaming. Is same as dead. True, memory is lovely—for old people—if they make eighty, ninety. You know."

Ann Aimsley sighed. "Imamu, she is my best friend—but a dangerous woman—that is, if you believe her. Thank God, you have a good head on your shoulders."

Holding the toothpick with his lips, Imamu laughed. He liked her saying that. He might be poor but he wasn't easy.

He thought back on Dora Belle's apartment. It was like Dora Belle—sexy and comfortable. No gleam of polish and cleanliness preserved in plastic here. The colors sucked you in. An orange plush couch welcomed the backsides with a hug that encouraged sitting. The rugs were dark brown; the walls, painted a pale orange, were hung with stuffed red and blue birds who looked ready to take off through the windows. Bowls of fruit had been set out, so that a flip of the wrist brought the best-tasting fruit to the mouth. The apartment created a need for laziness. Dora Belle's bedroom had a lounging chair and a big, soft, oversized bed. Perfume hung like a curtain in the air. Imamu was anxious to go back to it. He wanted to sit and sit and sit. So he was amazed at the sigh of relief that went through him when his foster mother said, "My God, where did the time go? Do you realize how late it is? I'm sorry, Dora Belle, but we have to leave."

"But you must come back soon." Dora Belle's fingers played along Imamu's arm. "You family. Perk and Gail does come and Peter does come. They like the comfort of me home. Except don't trouble me too early in the morning, and don't mess with me beauty sleep before dinner—that's how I does stay young, you know?" She smiled. "But come anytime—"

"Imamu," Ann Aimsley said impatiently, "what do you think we should have for dinner?"

"What about Chinese food?" He realized he was hungry again.

"Chinese food?" Dora Belle laughed. "You better bring your man home some pork chops or steak if you ain't want to look for another one."

"Chinese food!" Peter Aimsley said, picking up a fork. "Woman, where's my pork chops?" He began to push forkfuls of food into his mouth. "What kind of food is this to be giving a man after a hard day's work?"

"I thought we'd want to have something that Imamu liked on his first day with us," Ann Aimsley answered.

Peter Aimsley pointed his fork at Imamu. "This what you like, man?"

Imamu squirmed. He didn't care what he ate. Kentucky Fried, Arthur Treacher's, and McDonald's were his stick. He was a natural fast-food man. But Mrs. Aimsley ought to have known that her husband didn't go for Chinese food.

"Don't let these women pull this stuff on you, man." Peter Aimsley was smiling. "Tall as you are, you need meat and potatoes to fill you out. Women, they get scared over their waistlines and try to pass that jive on to us brothers."

Imamu realized that Peter Aimsley was trying to make up for the way he had acted that morning. He searched his mind for words for a give-and-take.

"Don't begrudge us Imamu's first meal," Ann Aimsley said. "It was a quick response to our problems. We overstayed ourselves at Dora Belle's."

"What you have to go there for?" Peter Aimsley asked. "She was here this morning. What you all got to say to one another twice a day that can't be said twice a month?"

"I suppose the same things that you and the kids have to say when you go there," Ann Aimsley answered with her pleasant smile.

"They went because of this morning," Perk chirped in, grinning wisely, and Imamu wondered why little kids thought that bare gums were so cute they had to keep showing them.

"This morning?" Ann Aimsley stared sternly at Perk, but Toothless only giggled.

"Because Godmother went for Imamu, that's why. Couldn't you tell? Gail said Godmother acted cheap—"

Gail flushed and lowered her eyes. She stared at her plate as Perk kept on. "I bet he liked her too—"

"Perk! What a thing to say." Mrs. Aimsley reached over to hold her talkative daughter's arm.

But Peter Aimsley laughed. "Well, if he likes her and she likes him, that's a damn good beginning. That's one fine woman, ain't she, boy? Got bread too. That's a gone combination. It ain't easy to come by. Go after it."

"Daddy!" Gail had been silent all during the meal. Now she looked angrily at her father. "What a sexist remark!"

"It certainly isn't a good example to set for your son," Ann Aimsley said.

Peter Aimsley looked hard at his plate, cowed. But before the silence could stretch out too long, he looked up at Imamu and winked. "Man, there ain't no win in a house full of women."

"And that's another one," Gail said, putting down her fork and looking at Imamu. "I hope you don't have those attitudes toward women."

Imamu swallowed. "Attitude? What attitude?"

"Sexist."

He stared at her. "Toward women?"

"Yes."

"Sure I got sexist attitudes toward women. What kind I'm supposed to have? I ain't no punk."

Peter Aimsley threw his head back and laughed loud, long. Gail jumped to her feet. "You dare to brag about it?"

"Gail, whatever is the matter with you?" Mrs. Aimsley stared at her daughter, perplexed. "I have never seen you get so upset—about nothing."

"You call it nothing?" she asked, her voice almost breaking.

"Sit down," Ann Aimsley ordered. Gail sat down, staring in front of her. "Whatever in the world is wrong with you? It's just possible that you and Imamu are talking about two different things."

"Why are you taking up for him?" Gail's eyes flashed. She was near to tears, but she didn't seem able to stop talking. "After all, the best way to get an understanding is through intelligent dialogue. Don't you agree?"

"Exactly, dear," her mother said. "But Gail, you must remember that Imamu has to get used to the way you say things."

"Why do you feel that you must talk for him, Mother? He's not retarded!"

"Gail! How dare you suggest . . ."

Imamu sat with his head bowed over his plate, wondering what had brought about the argument.

"To discuss is the only way to find out about each other," Gail cried.

"Of course it is, dear—"

"It is," Perk chimed in. "We ought to talk about everything and know everything about one another. Imamu, tell us, were you really innocent? Or did you kill that man?"

In the silence that followed, Imamu felt himself lean out of himself to strike at the grinning toothless mouth before him. But then he heard three voices cry out together: "Perk!" He had not moved.

Pushing back his chair, he ran out of the kitchen, ran up the stairs and out of the house into the street.

6

A red blur covered his eyes as he ran. But halfway down the block a sharp pain under his rib cage stopped him. He doubled up and leaned against a tree. He waited for the pain to pass but it only grew sharper. His breath pushed out of his lungs in painful spurts. He could feel the pulse beat at his temples. Sweat broke through his pores, wetting his shirt, which clung to him. With difficulty he unbuttoned his shirt so that the breeze found his bare chest. He waited. Minutes went by. A bird chirped in the tree. He heard the flow of cars on the street behind him. The red blur lifted; his breath eased. At last the pain stopped.

Imamu looked over the darkening, tree-lined street. What was he doing here in this strange land, far away from New York? Far from everything he had ever known? A stranger on foreign turf. Brooklyn. He bit his lips to keep down tears. What had he been doing in that house, with those people? What did they have to do with him? The tears kept pushing up. To stop them he hissed loudly to the tree, "What the hell was that chick talking about, anyway?"

Imamu flattened himself against the trunk of the tree and closed his eyes, glad that the leaves on the branches bowing over him were full enough to screen him from passers-by. It made him feel safe, protected from the world, away from life.

Slowly he let the scene at the dinner table replay through his mind. He saw Mrs. Aimsley, playing for time so he could get to know the family—and they could get to know him. Mr. Aimsley, trying to try. Perk, with her round face and gummy smile. He looked long at her face. He saw her bright eyes flashing her intention of being Perk, of being smart, open, letting her thoughts hang out. He sort of liked her: liked the fact that she didn't keep anything hidden—unlike Gail.

Gail dug him. He knew she did. Ever since he had walked into the house there was that between them. But she had to hide it behind being intelligent. She had to let him know she was intelligent. Why didn't she just come out and say it? No sweat. With those big, clear, brown eyes, that college-student style, he'd believe her. Hell, he'd believe anybody who told him they were intelligent. She didn't even have to prove it. He was the *street*, he knew that—a high school dropout who had dropped out even while he was sitting in class looking at the teacher. No problem. No problem at all. Why did she have to pull class on him? His face tightened.

"But ain't I see somebody foot under that tree?" A querulous voice broke into his thoughts. "But what it doing there? I see it, I tell you. It white, white like anything." The West Indian woman's voice brought Imamu out of the shadows. He started walking up the block, the voice behind him. "But who he? I ain't know he a-tall. Never see he before."

Imamu laughed bitterly. That told of his strangeness. He had never been on a tree-lined street with little houses, with people sitting in their chairs to air out, to rest. People's mouths turned into prunes at the sight of him, his naked chest; seeing him, they would remember him if they ever saw him again.

Yeah, he was a street dude. Even walking up a green-smelling heaven, with flower gardens ready to push into bloom, he represented the street. To these folks, tied together by their accents, by their plastic-covered houses, he brought the smell of fear, reminding them that they might have bought heaven, but heaven was not very far from the street. They hadn't gone nowhere: *He* was still there.

He took a toothpick out of his pocket, put it in his mouth, and felt better.

He ought to just quit the scene. Blow. There were things he didn't want to get used to. He didn't want to get used to people getting used to him, or to sitting at a dinner table to eat at eight o'clock because somebody else was hungry. It was damn uncivilized, the way he saw it—like the cavemen or like animals eating because someone threw them a bone.

He sure didn't want to get used to some chick being intelligent about sex. He had news for her. Sex around the dinner table in Brooklyn was the same as sex on Harlem street corners—or anywhere. Where did she get off trying to make sex heavy? He didn't want to prove anything. But she had a billion living proofs—more if she wanted to count birds, bees, and goddamn rats. There was plenty of proof if she wanted to find it. Hell, she could even find it in test tubes.

A group of boys turned the corner, headed toward Imamu. From their equipment, Imamu guessed they were part of a basketball team. When they reached the second stoop on the block, they stopped walking and crowded together, talking, shouting.

"You saw what happened," one yelled over the rest. "That cat fouled me."

"They got them big cats on their team," a second boy said. "They can overpower you, man."

"I still could have made it," the first boy shouted back. "But he fouled me."

A third said, "What we need is a couple of big guys. Tall. Guys who know how to play dirty."

Imamu stood at the curb, listening to them. They were all around his age—fifteen, sixteen—and about five seven, five nine. He kept standing there, waiting for them to turn, to see him, size him up. They didn't. On an impulse he spoke up.

"Where you dudes play?"

A quiet fell when they looked around to see who had spoken. They looked him over, his height, his clothes, his eyes. Then they shouldered together, feeling strength, Imamu knew, against him in their touching. One of them answered guardedly. "The center."

"What center?"

They nudged each other; they had told enough. Seeing they didn't want to answer, Imamu asked, "Near here?"

"Over at the church," the second boy said.

He wanted to ask what church. But because of their uneasiness, he asked again, "Near here?"

"Couple blocks." They stared at him with still eyes, waiting for the next question.

"Play every night?"

"Some nights."

"Where you dudes hang when you ain't playing?"

They exchanged uneasy glances. They didn't dig the sound of him, the feel of him, the feel of the street in him. "Mostly at each other's houses," the first boy said.

Imamu wanted to pressure them. What house? What's the number? What day are you where? Here? I got free time. I'm in the neighborhood. I can play, man. I can play. Instead, he stood looking as they edged away. One ran up the stoop where they had been standing. The others waited until he was inside—safe from him; then they walked down the block. Imamu had messed with their after-game excuses, their reasons for outshouting one another.

Rearing back on the curb, Imamu lowered his eyelids, feeling the boys as they went away from him, feeling their fear as they oozed into the approaching darkness, eased past the locks of their doors, and stood waiting, listening, wondering if they had left the street outside.

Twisting the toothpick around in his mouth, Imamu laughed in his throat. He began walking the block, in the direction in which they had disappeared. He wanted them to peer out of their doors, from behind their curtains, and see him walking. Let them know that, yeah, man, I'm here.

He walked down that block and the next. Then he found himself in the center of a buzz of folks. They were out in numbers—boys, girls. Not so many as in the city—brownstones didn't spew out as many bodies. But he heard loud talking and got the feeling of happenings. He stared back toward the place he had come from, wanting to go back, wanting to walk up that quiet street where the trees were planted so close together they acted as a shelter. He liked the feeling of being part of a full-grown tree. It was boss. Like, it gave you strength —strength rising from the roots. Damn. It was already becoming a habit, and the habit didn't just grow on you, it leaped at you.

Imamu didn't go back. He kept on ambling down the street. He turned a corner and stood still, catching strips of conversations. He wanted to attach himself to a group. But which group? Then he noticed an old brownstone in the process of being renovated. He had stumbled on to Dora Belle's street. They had come by car earlier, and he had not noticed how near she lived. Imamu walked down to the house she lived in and stood on the sidewalk, looking at the light-reddened windows. She had asked him to come—anytime, she had said.

The thought of the plush couch, the soft, brown-skinned woman, made a vein throb at his temples. An unthinking need drove him up the steps, but as his fingers reached for the bell he changed his mind. He had seen her twice already that day. Why rush things? Back down on the sidewalk, he walked quickly from the block and went in search of the nearest subway.

When he got there, his old neighborhood seemed to have changed during the day. It had become more dilapidated. His mother's building seemed more crushed than ever by the weight of the tenants who crowded the stoop. The hallway looked dimmer. He didn't want to go in. Suddenly he was offended by the smell of urine on the rickety steps he would have to climb to get to his mother's apartment. Still, he ought to go up to get his duffel.

It was dark now. The windows looked like empty faces glaring out over the heads of passers-by. No one's possessions, houses like this—not the tenants', not the landlords'. No one loved them. Folks moved in, planning on moving out, then stayed until they breathed their last. Landlords collected rents from houses that had earned out their original investment a hundred times—while letting the houses rot until they fell in upon their dead.

There were no lights at his mother's window, which meant nothing. She might be asleep. He ought to find out, to see if she was breathing. Anyway, he ought to go get his duffel. But he didn't.

Feeling guilty, Imamu tried to see his mother the way he had pictured her that morning—sweet-faced, clear-eyed, smelling of soap. Instead, her abused face, her accusing eyes haunted his thoughts. He smelled the sour liquor on her breath, seeping through her pores. God, what a long day.

On his way back to the subway, Imamu passed the old pool hall where he and his friends sometimes passed away the day. He looked in and saw familiar faces, people doing the same old things. He had never played much pool. He and his man Muhammed—and Iggy—hung at this corner. The corner felt lonely with them gone. Imamu reached into his pocket for a toothpick, then stood twirling it around in his mouth, his hands in his pockets.

Who had given Iggy that piece, he wondered. Everybody knew that Iggy was way out. Muhammed knew. Iggy was bad. He had broken mean since he had turned nine. He had started out stomping younger kids around the block. Then one day Imamu had caught him beating a stray cat over the head. "What you do that for, man?" he had asked.

"I'm just a bad nigger, that's why," Iggy had answered.

"Well, I ain't hanging with that kind of bad nigger," Imamu had told Iggy, "cause I love me some cats."

So Iggy had stopped beating cats. But one day Imamu had seen him slit the belly of a living dog. Imamu had gotten scared, sick. He had wanted to tell his mother. But by that time she was hitting the bottle.

Imamu had tried to stay away from Iggy. But Iggy loved Imamu. He had saved Iggy from the fire. So he was stuck with him. But the word was out on Iggy: he was crazy. No one with any sense would have walked into a store with Iggy, knowing he was carrying a piece. But he and Muhammed had walked into Fein's store with Iggy.

They had always hit Fein's store, for little things —potato chips, bread, salami, things they could take to the park or a show and eat.

Imamu had been slipping a bag of chips into his pocket that day when he had heard Iggy's voice. "Fein man, just hand over that bread."

"What you doing, man?" Imamu had asked him.

"What it look like he's doing?" Muhammed had answered. So Muhammed had known.

"Look, man." He had started right then to chicken out. Too late: he had heard that gun go off, had seen Fein's face. Iggy kept pulling that trigger, enjoying it.

Imamu had blacked out. Except he hadn't fainted. He came to his senses in the park, running, running like something wild. Then he had just gone on home to wait. Iggy wouldn't tell if they caught him. But Muhammed—he had never been one for much pain. He had sent The Man.

"Whatcha know, man?" Al Stacy came out of

the pool hall. "Thought that was you. Whatcha 'bout?"

"Nothing to me, man."

"Don't say? Too bad about Iggy and Muhammed."

"Yeah. Too bad."

"Hated what happened to old man Fein." Al Stacy spoke with contempt in his voice.

"Yeah."

"Lousy break. What get into you dudes?"

"Man, I didn't know Iggy had that piece—" It made no sense for Al Stacy to accuse him.

"You jiving? What got into you cats? Muhammed? He on smoke or he snorting?"

"Man, I don't know."

"Like, you don't know where Iggy got that piece—"

"No, man, I swear. I just looked around and—"

"That's a sick dude." Al Stacy looked down at his shining shoes. He was older than Imamu—twenty-six. A gambler, a stud, he philosophized with them but never hung with them. "Hell," he said, "ain't nothing in Fein's store worth his life."

"You right, man. You right." Imamu heard himself begging. Like, folks didn't believe him! "Man, I known Fein all my life. He gave me my first candy—"

"Hey, come on. You talking to Al Stacy. You jokers used to hit that old man's store just as soon as look at it."

"Nothing to mean nothing, man. Hell, Fein was my friend. He knew my old man, my old lady when—" Imamu thought of old man Fein's yellowed face, his bony fingers poking into his arm. "Such a lovely lady. What a shame. Why you don't take her to AA? Get help?"

Imamu shook his head to rid it of Fein and all the memories he'd shared with the old man.

He did most things with the guys. He had hit stores, supermarkets. He had been guilty as hell when he had served time for the break-and-enter. That had stopped him. He wanted to be in the streets, at home. He had his old lady to look after.

"They need to put that Iggy in the nuthouse so they can look inside his head," Al Stacy was saying. "Instead they gonna let him out so he can nut out again."

"They mightn't," Imamu answered.

"So what will they do? Let him stay in jail and kill a timer?"

"Ain't nothing they can do about dudes like Iggy," Imamu replied.

"You joking or are you like that for real?" Al Stacy stepped back to give him an all-over inspection. "Ain't nothing The Man can't do. If he want. He gone to the moon, ain't he? He flying like a bird in outer space, ain't he? Then how you figger he can't look into Iggy's simple head? Man, I figgered you out for more up there." He touched his head.

Imamu stood silently. It hurt bad when Al Stacy low-rated him. He ran at least second best to Stacy in terms of thinking. Yet here his teacher was putting him down, thinking that he knew more about Fein's killing than he was telling. His mother did, too. He thought of Ann Aimsley. There was one somebody who believed him.

"Hey, man, got to split," he said. "Got some folks in Brooklyn I just got to see." Hitching up his shoulders, he swaggered carelessly away. Then he turned the corner and almost ran to the nearest subway.

7

Imamu let himself quietly into the house, then ran up the steps to his room. "Come in here!" He heard Peter Aimsley's voice and stopped to listen. Who was he talking to? "Do you hear me, boy?" Imamu flipped all those in the house who might be called boy through his mind. He came nearest that description. But he was tired, real tired; he didn't want to talk to anyone, not even Ann Aimsley. "I said come in here!"

Imamu backed down the steps and walked toward the living room. Peter Aimsley met him at the door. "Where you been?" he asked. Imamu stilled the panic that rose in him at the sight of the broad shoulders, the angry face. Ann Aimsley stood near the window, her face showing signs of distress. Had something happened while he was out? "I'm talking to you, boy. Answer me!"

"Out," Imamu answered.

"I ain't asked because I thought you was in. Out where?"

Both Mr. and Mrs. Aimsley were dressed for bed, so something terrible must have happened. Or—the thought struck him—were they waiting for him? "Just out," he said.

What did the cat think? Just because he had come to live there he was ready to slide back to lollipops? Imamu kept himself tuned to any sudden moves of the thick, muscled arms, the clenching and unclenching fists, ready to duck or feint if required.

"In this house," Peter Aimsley said, "we don't just go out. In this house we are responsible to one another. In this house we know where one another is at all times. Now I'm asking one more time. Where you went?"

Imamu kept his eyes on the older man's fists. What to say to that? He had been out. By himself. Walking the streets. Riding the trains. It was his business. But if he told that to the dude, there'd be trouble. "Out with friends."

"What friends?"

Imamu shook his head, not believing what he heard. He laughed in his throat. This man had to be kidding. What did he call this? Father and son routine? Did he think he was going to pick Imamu's friends? "My friends," he repeated.

"Yeah, yeah, I heard that. But I want to know who they are. Where they are. Where they live."

"That ain't none of your business."

Before he knew what was happening the hands

had reached out and snatched him by the collar. He felt Peter Aimsley's breath hot on his face. "In this house everything is my business. You get that?" Imamu was the taller of the two, yet held in the man's hands, he felt weak, vulnerable. "I don't have to stay." His voice quivered. Peter Aimsley pushed him from him.

"Help yourself. But if you stay here, believe me, it's like I say it is."

"Then you got it." Imamu pushed anger into his quavering voice. He turned to leave, but Ann Aimsley came up to him and held his arm.

"Imamu, please— Listen. Your—Mr. Aimsley was so worried. I was, too. We had no idea what had happened to you. All we ask is that you let us know—"

Then why hadn't she told him before? Why had she let him think that he could come and be himself and everything would be fun? Hell, she had to know himself was from the street, that her man was antistreet. At least give him a choice!

He wanted to push her out of his way, go through her to the door. But he could not bring himself to touch her, be rough to her. The unhappiness in her face, her body thrust between him and escape, made him want to fall into her arms, cry on her shoulder. If she had deceived him, it hadn't been her intention.

"I was in Harlem," he said.

"Oh, you see, Peter"—she put her hand through his arms, turned him to face her husband—"that's why he is so late. You know the time trains make at night."

"What in the hell was he doing in Harlem? He just left there this morning! Let me tell you one thing"—Peter Aimsley pointed his finger at Imamu—"Harlem is a place you don't have to go as long as you live here. And another thing, when you're out and it gets two o'clock in the morning, stay out. Nobody brings me that kind of time."

"Bring you? Who you?" Imamu felt Ann Aimsley's arm restraining his shaking body.

"I'm the one who sets time in this house."

"Not for me," Imamu cried. "I ain't no baby."

"You damn right you ain't. That's why you got to listen. Hell, when I was your age I was getting up at this time. To go to work. I own the place now! Dig it? Sixteen when I started out and I own the place. So I know you ain't no baby. Tell it to her." He jerked his thumb at his wife.

"Peter, let's not keep shouting. Imamu has just come. He has to get used to us."

"Then he'd better hurry. That's the second time you said that today. If by the third time he ain't used to us, he don't stay."

Blood rushed to Imamu's face as he realized that Gail and Perk were standing outside the living room door. Then to add to his shame, the outside door opened and Mr. Elder came to stand in the shadow under the stairs, his black coat blending into the darkness, his eyes glistening strangely white under the cliff of his brow.

Peter Aimsley brushed by Imamu and Ann Aimsley on his way to the stair. "If you go out that door this night, make sure you keep going. If you stay, know this. I ain't about to change. In this house I'm the man. That ain't nothing to get used to, boy. That's something that is!"

Ann Aimsley kept her hand on his arm. "Imamu," she said, "don't let tonight spoil things. Peter is upset. I'm upset. After all, we know what trouble young boys get themselves into out there. We couldn't help but worry. Let's all get some sleep. Things will be better tomorrow."

Imamu's heart jerked at her words. Maybe it was the smell of the soap in her hair that quieted his protest. Maybe it was the thought of the apartment house he hadn't wanted to go into or the long subway ride. He had traveled so long, so far to get back. He didn't want to leave. And the shame of not wanting to leave struggled with his anger. So when Perk came up to him with her toothless grin and said, "I bet I know where you went tonight, and I bet it wasn't in nobody's Harlem—" he turned on her.

"I got enough of your big mouth," he said. "Just shut up! Shut up and stay the hell on out of my way!"

But the next morning it was Perk who woke him up, early. "Get up, get up, Imamu." Her voice reached him as though from a long distance. She kept shaking him. He tried to open his eyes. His eyelashes were stuck together. "Will you get up?" Her insistent voice forced him to peel apart his lashes. He looked up into the impish grin. "I want you to button my dress," she said, turning her back to him.

Imamu closed his eyes, refusing to believe what he had heard. "Ain't this a shame?" He turned his back to her and pulled the covers over his head. But the quiet in the room turned him over, and he sat up, leaning on one elbow, and tried to get the buttons in the right buttonholes.

"Hurry up. I'll be late."

"Look," he grumbled, "don't be waking me up for jive stuff like this." Nevertheless he worked at the buttons.

"Why not?" she asked. "Everybody else in the house is up."

"What's that got to do with me?"

"How do you expect to get used to the family if all you do is sleep?"

Imamu finished buttoning the dress and pushed her away. Did the girl ever keep her mouth shut? When she turned to him and looked at him with her bright golden eyes, he realized that she had awakened him to say that she liked him. He looked over the yellow dress, with yellow birds embroidered on it, her yellow socks pulled neatly up from her white shoes to her chubby knees, and said, "Do you go to school looking like that all the time?" She was pretty, pretty and golden.

"We have a party today," Perk answered. "Then there's a holiday. Can you take me somewhere for the holiday?"

"Like where?"

"Anywhere."

Before he had a chance to answer, Ann Aimsley called, "Perky, what are you doing? Will you come on so that I can comb your hair?"

Perk ran from the room, then stuck her head back in and with a return of her impish grin said, "You going to turn into a vegetable if you don't get your lazy butt up." Imamu threw a pillow at the closing door. A piece of yellow satin ribbon, which Perk had left on the bed, fell to the floor. He lay looking at it, wanting to get up and take it down to her. But he just lay there, looking at the ribbon and thinking of her.

He was glad she had come. She had somehow taken some of the shame out of the night—made his argument with Peter Aimsley feel like a family argument, like the arguments he had seen on TV, in the movies. Then he remembered what Ann Aimsley had said about his getting into trouble. But she had just been talking off the top. She hadn't meant what she said. He covered his head and tried to force himself back to sleep. He grew wider and wider awake. What trouble did she think he would get himself into?

He lay there, looking up at the ceiling, forcing himself to lie still, waiting, wanting everyone to leave before he got up. It was a comfortable bed, clean. He enjoyed the lingering smell of Clorox in the sheets. He enjoyed the look of the room. It was not as large as his room uptown, but it looked larger because it was uncluttered, clean, the walls white, the furniture plain. The bedclothes were a joy to lie between—the sheets, the satin-bordered blanket, the blue chenille bedspread. The dresser and chest were painted, or stained, a deep brown. They were empty, waiting for his things. If he was allowed to stay.

A sudden impatience forced him out of bed. When he looked past the thin white curtains at the street, he saw that it was almost deserted. The cars that had lined the curb the night before had vanished. He looked around for his clothes: the same shirt he had worn the day before, the pants he had worn for two days. He had to get back to Harlem for his duffel. Today. No matter what the old man said.

Putting on his pants, Imamu listened for sounds from below. He went out of the room and stood at the top of the stairs. The house was silent. He walked down the carpeted steps on bare feet and listened at the door which led down to the kitchen. Silence. Everyone must have gone.

In the living room he looked around; then he saw the stereo set. He hadn't noticed it the day before. He searched around for records and found them on shelves behind the couch, just beneath the big painting. Instead of going through the records, he looked at the painting.

If anything, the painting seemed larger than it had the day before, more powerful. Facing it, he seemed rather to be standing under it, looking up, waiting for the great wave to break over him and crush him. At closer range the dark shadows beneath the foam were matchstick figures of people—heads, legs, arms, sticking out—waiting for the wave to crush them.

"Do you like that painting, Imamu?" Ann Aimsley had come into the room and began setting out ashtrays. He turned to look at her and was relieved that her face appeared as good, as calm, as it had before. Somehow, lying upstairs in bed, thinking of her, he had imagined that her face had been marked by doubts, fears.

"Yes, ma'am."

"One of my roomers—when I had roomers—painted it."

"Somebody painted that! I mean—somebody you know?"

"It took him a long time. Almost the entire time he stayed here—six years."

Imamu looked in wonder at the painting. "That long?"

"That's what he *said* he was doing all that time."

"And he *gave* it to you?"

"For two years' rent."

"Whee." Imamu whistled. "All that work! And he just gave it to you?"

"For two years' rent," Ann Aimsley reminded him. "Then he had to move."

"And you just took it?"

"When he left he was still owing me. I appreciate

that people do get involved in their art, but we all have to pay our way."

Imamu looked at her dusting the dustfree furniture, arranging things that were already arranged, picking up specks—one of them a broken piece of toothpick—from the carpet, then stepping back to admire her efforts. He tried to imagine her actually taking a painting from some dude who had taken six years to paint it. He pictured her holding the painting behind her while a hand was stuck out in front demanding the rest of the change. He shook his head. Not her.

"I'll be going out," she said, "leaving the house to you. Look around. Get acquainted with things. Relax. Fix whatever you want for breakfast. Just make sure you clean up after yourself. Everything is there. Coffee is made. Milk, eggs, what have you, in the fridge. I'll be home in time to make dinner about five." And he had thought she had doubts about him!

"Let's make it a family evening." She smiled. "You'll like us, Imamu. You really will."

She walked to the door, then said: "I'll leave money. Buy yourself a few shirts. We'll do our big shopping on the weekend." She waited for an answer. He tried to say thanks but couldn't. He hated himself for having had doubts about her.

She started upstairs, then stopped. "It's all right for you to go and give Dora Belle a hand, if you want. Just make sure she doesn't keep you."

"What makes you think I'm going there?" Imamu

asked. He hated it that she had killed the excitement of the thought.

Ann Aimsley laughed. "Dora Belle has that effect —on you men. Just you be sure you eat dinner at home." She went upstairs.

The clean kitchen filled him with guilt when he walked in. He hated messing it up with cooking. For a moment he thought of going over to Dora Belle and having her fix his breakfast. No. Today, he was all about following some instructions.

Opening the refrigerator, Imamu got an attack of the jumps, like he was about to hit a supermarket. It was crammed. He decided on bacon, eggs, jam, bread, and milk. The cupboard was another trip. Cans were stacked so tight that he had to fight to get one can of anchovies loose, then had to spend five minutes restacking the others so he could close the door.

While the bacon was cooking, he looked around for dishes. This was another experience. One shelf held only plates, another held only saucers, and still another only cups. One cabinet had only glasses: shelves and shelves of glasses. It was wild. He and his mother had been substituting jars for glasses for the past few years—jam jars, peanut butter jars, mayonnaise jars, jars, jars.

His new family had it made. How rich were they? As rich as Dora Belle? No, Dora Belle had three houses—and no kids.

He broke a pair of eggs on top of the bacon. He'd leave his milk until after breakfast. It had been a long time since he had used a glass. He didn't drink wine, whiskey, or beer, and he took his soda from the bottle. But this morning—the first in his new home—he intended to wrap his lips around expensive stuff. He slipped the bacon and eggs onto a plate and sat down.

After he had eaten, Imamu washed and wiped his plate and fork and the pan, put them away, and then went to choose the glass he wanted to drink from. Standing on a chair, he searched the shelves, noticing that the higher the shelf, the more expensive the glasses looked. Those on the top shelf were made of heavy cut crystal. Some of them had long stems. From among these he choose a wine glass and took it to the table. He poured out his milk, then took a jar of cherries from the refrigerator and added enough syrup to turn the milk a deep pink. He sat down ready to enjoy.

Then he remembered the stereo set. He left the milk, went to the living room, turned on the player, then look through the records. Finding some old numbers—which he had expected—he put on some of Max Roach's and some of Randy Weston's, and went back to the kitchen. Rearing back in his chair, he snapped his fingers and patted his feet to the beat of the music. He felt go—od.

He had done a boss job of cooking breakfast. The place was as clean as when he had started. He deserved an A for really being together.

He finished his milk and washed and dried the glass. Reaching to put it in its place on the shelf, he looked over his shoulder to make sure the table was clean. As he took his hand away, the glass tipped over.

He saw it falling and grabbed for it. It broke against the sink, shattering into hundreds of pieces. One piece cut deep into the heel of his right hand. Blood spurted from the cut over the sink, onto the wall, and dripped on the floor. He had to have cut an artery! Imamu grabbed a towel and wrapped it around his hand. Then he picked up the biggest pieces of glass from the sink with his left hand and put them into a brown paper bag in the cabinet under the sink. Turning on the water full force, he flushed the splinters down the drain.

By this time blood had soaked through the towel. He snatched a wad of paper towels and put it in place of the bloody towel, which he threw into the bag along with the broken glass. He washed the blood off the walls, the sink, and the floor, and when he had finished, he glanced up at the glasses in the cabinet. His heart almost stopped when he saw the space left by the missing glass. He stood on a chair and reshuffled the rest of the glasses to fill the empty space. Then he went upstairs to the living room and turned off the player. He ran up to his room and put on his shirt, then went back down to the kitchen. Taking the brown paper bag with the glass and bloody towel, he left the house.

Mr. Elder was coming up the stoop as Imamu started down. He looked at Imamu, then at his bandaged hand, then cleared his throat with a loud *hurrumph*. Imamu started to explain, but changed his mind and turned his head away from the piercing look; he scooted down the steps and hurried down the block.

Why explain to Frankenstein? He would have enough explaining to do where it counted. God, it seemed that everything he had done since he got to this house had turned out a bust.

8

Dora Belle had said to come at any time, but she was not at home. Imamu kept ringing her bell. Her car was parked at the curb, and he could hear music coming from inside the house. Why didn't she answer? Did she have someone in there? Had she been making believe she dug him when all the while she was into somebody else? Imamu bit his bottom lip to stop it from trembling. He felt small and alone.

Things had happened so fast this morning. There he had been, having a ball, worrying about nothing, naturally goofing—an accepted member of a family. He had everything going for him, and then one broken glass and he was right back out here, alone and bleeding.

He considered going up to Harlem. But the thought of walking through the smelly hallway, sitting in the messy apartment turned him off. He'd be alone there, too. Or worse: His mother might be in her room sleeping, drunk, while he was sitting in his, bleeding to death.

Still, there were no glasses there too precious to break, no ashtrays too clean for ashes or broken toothpicks. At home the floors were not too spotless to receive his blood. In that lack of care there was an amount of safety.

Cradling his swaddled hand to his chest, Imamu walked down to the sidewalk and stood looking around at the rows of brownstones. He knew that there were no doorbells that he could ring to say, "Look, I cut my hand." No, he was a stranger with the smell of the street on him.

Reluctantly, he walked up the block, expecting any moment she would open the door and call him back. He stood halfway between her two other houses, waiting for tenants who might come in or go out, wanting to inquire who had seen Dora Belle. Only twice did the door of her second house open. Both times the persons—one a man, the other a woman—looked suspiciously at Imamu and both times they hurried away, discouraging questions. As Imamu stood uncertainly, wondering if he should go across the street to the empty house, he saw her coming out of it.

She looked different, almost ordinary. Her head was wrapped with a black cloth; a gray, loose-fitting smock hid her figure. Wearing flat shoes, she just didn't fit the picture that he had of her. Or perhaps the idea of her in work clothes, with soiled hands, hadn't occurred to him.

He crossed the street to meet her. But she didn't

look up at his approach. And when he walked right up to her, her hands went to her heart in fright at being approached by a stranger. Then she recognized him.

When she finally spoke it was to cry angrily, "Oho, so is now you come? All morning, all morning so, I got me grief. Work on me shoulder. And is now you bring your arse?"

Had she been expecting him? He searched his mind for the signals he had missed. She hadn't made them clear. "All morning, all morning so—" She raised her voice, so that people walking by stopped to listen, to take her side, nodding their heads in agreement. "I fix boiler, I take out bags of garbage big enough to kill a man—all by myself. Them mothers' children born without name done haul arse and leave me flat, flat, flat." She waved her hand toward the empty house. "The money I done pay to they, I could done build a big house and become millionaire. I tell you, all morning, all morning this does happen, that does happen. Me, woman lone, and is now you come? What you want?"

"I cut my hand," he said in a small boy's voice.

That quieted her, surprised her. She looked at him in amazement. After a long while she said: "Oho, so you cut your hand." He bowed his head. "And so? You dead?" She walked away toward her apartment. He followed, like a small boy.

And in the house he felt like a small boy. She unwrapped his hand. The cut was still bleeding.

She let water run on it. The blood kept coming. "Squeeze down hard," she said, putting his thumb over the cut. "Squeeze hard, hard, hard. I coming." Then she left him sitting in the living room while she went to dress.

He heard the water running in the bathroom. She was taking a shower while he sat bleeding! He wanted to leave, really wanted to go. But he sat on, squeezing down on his cut. The hands of the clock on the wall moved slowly. It made a complete hour's turn and he still sat. The cut had stopped bleeding.

"Well, I ready." She walked into the room, changed back into the person he knew. She wore a polished cotton dress that came to her knees. Her feet were thrust into high-heeled backless slippers, and the long silky curl draped down over her shoulder.

"So you cut your hand." She smiled her even-teeth smile and gave a prideful thrust to her high bosom as she laid medication and bandages down on the coffee table. "Let me see." She took his hand. The skin had closed together. It was, after all, a small cut, not more than a quarter of an inch long.

"That ain't look bad at all," she said. "When I see your face, I did think your hand cut off."

"It was bleeding bad."

"You done stick an artery," she said. "But it okay."

She poured iodine on the cut and bandaged his hand neatly with gauze. He sat looking at her, feeling stupid now that the bleeding had stopped. But he wondered why a small cut like that had made him feel so defeated.

"There now," she said. "You see? You ain't dead. What happen?"

"I broke a glass," he said. "One of Mrs. Aimsley's good glasses. A heavy one all cut out—"

"What!" Her eyes widened. "You mean to tell me you break one a Ann's good crystal? The one she hide all the way on the top of her closet, safe from people hands? The ones what she saving to look at the rest of she life? How come you reach all the way up there to break it?"

"That's me." He smiled feebly.

"Oh, God, man, you in trouble."

"I cut my hand bad trying to catch it."

"But Ann will cut off your head." Then realizing he didn't take that as a joke, she added: "Never mind she. You always have a home." She leaned toward him, her mouth parted, her eyes shining. Imamu blushed, turned away.

"But you ain't no baby."

No, he was no baby. That was sure. He smiled to hide his confusion, put his arm around the back of the couch. She twisted up under his armpit. The arm fell around her shoulders, his hand rested lightly on the swell of her bosom. "What happened to your gold locket?" he asked.

"Me? I ain't one to wear one man thing when I after the next." Meaning deepened her eyes. His eyes rushed from hers in panic. She forced them back, looked through them, her black slanting eyes searching for his soul. A feeling of apprehension caught at his stomach.

"Ain't you all engaged?"

"That Jacques! But where he is? I waiting long. Why I must wait? I a young woman," she said. "Lovely. I keep meself that way for me man—and I ain't mind paying the price for he. Why I must be alone? I ain't want to be alone—" Her eyes sucked him in. He wanted to snatch himself away. Run. Never stop running. She leaned against him. His arm fell down around her waist. He squeezed the soft flesh. No bones. He felt himself sinking into her soft flesh. A warmth stirred in the pit of his stomach.

Yet a part of himself moved away from her and curled into a ball inside of him, protecting him from her. What was he going to do with her? If he could pull away, he'd run, go, never stopping until he was safe in his room in Harlem. And all the while a voice inside him kept up a chant: "Chicken! Turkey!" Dora Belle pressed against him, raised her head. So he lowered his, brought his dry mouth down to meet her soft lips. The doorbell rang.

"Oh, God, me cross." Dora Belle jumped to her feet. "Everybody know the time when not to come. And so is the time they does come."

Weak with relief, Imamu got up and followed her into the foyer. He had to get out. Somewhere in his mind he knew he really wanted to stay—bad. But not as bad as he wanted to go.

Dora Belle had opened the door and a voice from

the other side was complaining: "Why is it that
every time I got to take a shower, I got to come to
your damn door? I get sick and tired—"

"Well, move!" Dora Belle shouted. "What you
want from me life? Well, you ain't getting it. All
you does waste me good water, waste me oil, waste
me time. You ain't like it here? Pack up and go,
nuh—"

She slammed the door, turned, and bumped into
Imamu. "See what I does suffer?" she cried.

"I got to go, Dora Belle."

She didn't seem to hear him. "Is so me life,
Imamu. Nobody helping me. Come, let me show
you." She hooked his hand and guided him out of
her apartment and up the stairs. "I does need somebody to vacuum these steps and polish these ban-
nisters from top to bottom, every day. What? You
think me life easy?"

He didn't know. He didn't want to know. All he
wanted to do was to make tracks getting out. She
led him back down and he breathed with relief
when, instead of going into her apartment again,
she went down to the apartment below, the garden
apartment. She took him out into the garden. "This
ground need turning, flowers need planting, and no
one lift a finger. Weeds growing like trees."

They went down to the cellar. ". . . I does set it
so, you see?" She showed him how to work the
thermostat. "When they does use it up they must
wait for it to hot. I ain't giving another cent more.
Oil does cost, you know. And here"—she led him

to the sink, where a hose was attached—"this to wash off the sidewalk. All you got to do is turn the water so. Same thing in me next house."

"Sweetheart." She flashed a smile. "If you does want money to do these little things, ax for it, nuh. But as you see, it ain't nothing. Anyway, you know the house is yours."

All the while she had been explaining, showing him around, Imamu kept his mind busy. Suddenly the best reason in the world came. So easy, so true. "Dora Belle, I got to split. Got to make it on up to Harlem to get my vines. See what I mean?"

"Vines?"

"Clothes, man, clothes."

"You coming back?" She rubbed her fingers along his spine.

He took out a toothpick, put it in his mouth, and smiled around it. "You asking? How you figger I can stop myself?" He felt happy; he had found himself again.

Somehow the smell of the urine in the hallway didn't turn him off the way it had the day before. He let himself into the apartment and stood with his back to the door, letting the decay, the smell of stale wine go through him, making it a part of him, so he could push it away. Nor did it matter as much when he found his mother was not at home. The usual catch in his chest, that mixture of love, pity, pain, did not happen. Maybe it was because too much had been going around in him, confusing him. It was sure he had run like a deer from Dora Belle. That, after she had given his manhood a real leap forward.

He sat on the edge of his mother's bed. He wanted to see her, his old lady. He had known her always; the familiar need for her haunted him. He missed being with her, making sure she was all right. Yet, when he had been in the lock-up, she had gone on just the same. What if he could open up a new world for her? A world of three houses—?

He sighed, got up, and went into the kitchen. The old refrigerator was, as always, foodless. So were the cupboards; he closed the doors quickly. There had been a time when they had had glasses.

The duffel bag lay on the floor just as he had left it. That gave him a strange feeling. It was as though he had died, leaving his things behind—things that would stay and stay, quietly, without meaning, as though the world had moved away. He hoisted the duffel onto his shoulder and left the apartment.

Once on the street he went to the supermarket up the avenue and, with the money Mrs. Aimsley had given him for shirts, bought a loaf of bread, some cheese and bologna. Outside the store he ripped open the packages to make sure they could not be returned. Then he went looking for someone to deliver them.

And as though he had called her up, Gladys Dawson came running down the street calling, "Hey, Imamu, wait up." As she came up to him, she said,

"Heard you was out. Been looking all over for you."

"Seen my mother?" he asked.

"Around."

"Do me one?" And at her nod he pushed the bag of groceries into her arms. "Get these to her for me."

"Whatcha into?" she asked.

"Got somebody to meet."

"Gonna take long? Happenings tonight."

"Can't say," he answered, shrugging.

"Imamu, man, I been missing you."

He laughed, grabbed her arm playfully. But at the feel of her thick, firm flesh bouncing back into his hand like rubber, he felt a stirring at the pit of his stomach for the second time that day. "Hey, baby." Suddenly she looked different to him. Good.

He had long outgrown Gladys as a type. Short, plump, tough-looking, the survival type. They had been young together. Real young. They had made the park scene together, the tall grass scene, the rooftop scene. She had looked wild back then, with her blouse going one way, her skirt the other, and her hair going all different ways.

Now, she had it all together. The suit she wore was a way-out two piece, the skirt short enough to show off her big legs. She wore false eyelashes and knew how to flirt with them. Her hair was pulled away from her face and drawn into a sleek pony-tail that bobbed sexily when she tossed her head.

"Whatcha do to yourself?" he asked. "You sure

looking good." He knew that she had never outgrown liking him.

"Glad you notice," she answered. "What about
tonight?"

"Tell me the place," he asked. He might make
the effort.

"My place. Promise you coming?"

"Well, I sure ain't said no," he answered. "Fine
as you look—"

He pulled playfully at her ponytail. Then for the
second time that day the unexpected happened:
Gladys jerked her head away. He looked down, saw
the ponytail in his hand, and looked up just in time
to see her fist coming at him. He stepped back and
got it full force in his chest. She pushed the groceries
back at him. They spilled over the sidewalk as he
grabbed his chest. Snatching her ponytail from him
she ran down the street. Imamu kept holding his
chest.

Someone behind him laughed. "I seen that. Now,
I know you known better than that, Imamu." Al
Stacy was standing in a doorway.

Tears stung Imamu's eyes. He tried to laugh.
"Man," he said, "that chick's got a fist like a man."

"Sure look like it from where I stand." Al Stacy
kept laughing.

"All I did was tell her she looking fine."

"That she does. Like she got all her stuff pulled
together yesterday. But Imamu, you got to know
you don't mess with no black chick's wigs. Never
mess with her wig and never mess with her money

—even when she gives it to you. A dude can get killed over that."

Al Stacy kept looking after Gladys; seeing how heavy for her the dude was, Imamu remembered that he had to be in Brooklyn for dinner.

"Got to run, man," he said. "Got to get these grits to the old lady and be making time." Stuffing his groceries back into the paper bag, Imamu heaved his duffel onto his shoulder and took off toward the apartment house.

9

Back in Brooklyn, Imamu let himself into the house. When he smelled the aroma of food coming up from the kitchen, he dropped his duffel bag and ran downstairs. Ann Aimsley looked up from washing vegetables. "Imamu!" she cried, surprised. "How good that you came home early." That was weird. She had asked him to come early. Hadn't she expected him to? "What happened to your hand?" she asked.

"Cut it." He answered. Then, before she could ask more, he added, "Dora Belle bandaged it for me."

"Is it bad?"

"Naw, just a scratch. Gail home yet?"

"She's upstairs changing. She'll be right down." Smiling, Ann Aimsley looked at him, trying to see through his expression. "You two have to know each other better. Gail's really a lovely girl. Perk, too. She talks a lot but she doesn't mean to be rude—just devilish. You'll get used to her."

Imamu sat at the table and watched Ann Aimsley moving around the kitchen. She went to the oven, opened it, and looked at her roast. "Leg of lamb," she said. Then she went back to the sink. The cotton house dress that she wore made her look younger, smaller, sweeter. But Imamu didn't know if he liked her that way. She didn't seem so sure of herself—not as impressive.

It was her smart appearance, Imamu was sure, that had convinced the judge to release him in her custody. In her smart suit, with her silk blouses, she had impressed him, too. Every day he had waited for the door to open and for her to walk in. It made every day special. It was unreal. Why should this well-dressed lady think him important enough to waste time on?

"Did you buy the shirts?" she asked.

"No, ma'am. I—I went up to Harlem." Funny, how guilty he felt going against her husband's wishes. "Had to pick up the rest of my things, you know? Then I got some stuff for the house—food."

"Oh? How is your mother?"

He wanted to lie, say all right. Instead he answered, "She was out—somewhere. I left the stuff in the house."

"I'm sorry," she said. He shrugged. "Have you talked to her at all—since the trial?"

"Some."

"Did she say why she never came?"

Irritation forced sweat to jump out at the back

of his neck. Why did she have to ask all those questions? She knew what was happening with his mother. "She ain't always together—know what I mean?"

Imamu wished she'd shut up about his mother. Let him feel relaxed. He wanted to rear back in his chair, put his feet on the table, and look at her. She shook every leaf of lettuce out of the water and put it in the towel, never getting a drop of water on the floor. Like she did everything with care. It sure paid off. Her house was a palace, her kids looked good—like they were something. Yet she had made it to court every day. She did her thing and still got home in time to get the grits going. Somewhere in that there had to be a lesson.

"I think it's a crime to let people go around sick —people with problems like your mother. They ought to be put somewhere to be cared for."

"She got to want to." He repeated what he had heard social workers say dozens of times.

"But if she's sick, how can they expect her to want to?"

"She been in the hospital," Imamu said. "They took her in once when they found her stoned in the park. They kept her then. But she had to come out —sometime. She joined the AA once, too—never kept up—"

"Maybe she had no reason to want to." Imamu looked at Ann Aimsley, surprised. That, too, went with her house dress. Did she hear what she had said? The lady looked serious. Didn't he look like a reason—a damn good reason?

"But then"—Ann Aimsley rambled on—"it seems to me I read somewhere that alcoholism—that type—might be an allergy. Something in the system, in certain types of people. They might never have even had one drink—then that one, and the system reacts—"

Imamu's interest peaked. That made sense. Winos didn't have a thing in common with hard drinkers he knew from around the streets. For one thing, winos all looked alike. Their faces flowed together, whether they were white, black, green, or purple—even those simple men he chased from around his mother looked like her around the muscles of their faces.

"I can't remember exactly where I read it—some magazine." Ann Aimsley became more vague as she went on. "I just seem to remember . . ."

That kind of talk went with the house dress. If she had on her other togs, she would have remembered the name and date of the magazine, even the place where she read it.

Restlessness made Imamu twist around in the chair. He wanted to know more. The sense of what she had said reminded him in a way of Al Stacy talking about Iggy—of him being crazy. Ideas he could be collecting to read up on, to know more about—when he started reading.

"Whom did you stay with when your mother was in the hospital?" Mrs. Aimsley asked.

"By myself."

"By yourself! How old were you?"

"Nine, ten, somewhere in there."

That was the time he had started looking after her, cooking for her, for himself, sometimes for Iggy. Campbell soups, Campbell pork and beans, hot dogs, hamburgers—all before the quickie chains got into the neighborhood.

"It must have been hard."

Now you said it, lady, hard. On us, not them. Ain't nothing hard about bending the elbows, copping out, or taking the needle and nodding. It's us who stand around holding the hands, smelling the vomit, messing with reality. We the ones hurting. All they doing is dying.

But he said, "She the one killing herself."

"It's strange that you didn't get on drugs. So many boys—"

"Ma'am, I'm a Muslim." He spoke quietly.

"Whatever the reason. I'm proud—"

"Hello." They hadn't heard Gail coming down the steps. Now she sauntered into the kitchen, dressed in jeans and a sport shirt, looking like early morning. Imamu reached into his pocket for a toothpick to have something to do with his face while he dug where she was really coming from.

"Where's Perk?" she asked.

"She hasn't come home yet."

"From school! She's pretty late, isn't she?"

"Probably stopped home with Babs."

Avoiding Imamu's eyes, Gail went to the closet and brought down a salad bowl. Imamu smiled around his toothpick. She talked big, but she was shy as a schoolgirl.

"I'll do that, Gail. Go and talk to Imamu," Mrs. Aimsley said. Gail went to sit across from Imamu, but her eyes went to his hand instead of his face.

"What happened to your hand?" she asked.

Imamu looked at her, his smile deepening around the toothpick. Mrs. Aimsley answered for him. "He cut his hand over at Dora Belle's. She bandaged it."

Gail reached over to turn his hand over. "Professional job," she said. "I'm glad to see Aunt Dora can do one thing well."

"Dora Belle does many things quite well," her mother said.

"I don't know any," Gail said.

"Gail, whatever in the world do you mean?" Ann Aimsley looked at her daughter in surprise.

"I mean that Imamu has been here for only two days, and he's been over there both days." Hearing the jealousy in her voice, Imamu took out the toothpick. He stared at her, trying to force her to look at him. He wanted to nail her. Let her know that he knew where she was coming from. But Gail kept her face turned from his, and he put his toothpick back in his mouth.

Ann Aimsley asked, "What is wrong with Imamu giving your godmother a hand? She's going to pay him, I'm sure."

"Aunt Dora pay? With what?"

"Don't be vulgar, Gail." Ann Aimsley looked at her sternly. "Imamu has nothing to do right now and—"

"What year are you in, Imamu?" Gail brushed

her mother's explanation aside and finally looked at Imamu. Now she felt in control. Imamu shook his head, wondering if he ought to feel angry at her or play it for laughs.

"I'm not," he answered.

"You're not? I mean what year were you in when you decided not to go on?"

"Junior."

"Well, that's not too bad." She smiled patronizingly. "Have you decided what subjects you are going to take when you go back?"

"Uh-uh." He hadn't said he was going back. No one had even asked him. So why did Ann Aimsley and her daughter assume that he was? There had to be more to life than wasting time in classrooms watching a bunch of cats blow hard against teachers who didn't know how to keep them in line.

"It will be difficult," Ann Aimsley said. "Schools are so backwards nowadays. When I was coming up in Harlem, even a word like ain't was forbidden. Today, teachers just don't care—"

"What do you want to be—" Imamu waited to hear Gail say "when you grow up." But she caught the look in his eyes and repeated, "What do you want to be?"

He studied her from under lowered lids. Did she dig him, or did her up-tight manner mean she didn't think him good enough? Not enough book-learning?

"A scientist," he answered, twisting his tooth-pick to the corner of his mouth.

"A—" Her eyes darkened as she realized he was

baiting her. "Really? How nice," she said. "I suppose at your age—"

"What do you want to be?" he asked, cutting her off.

"A fashion designer," she answered.

"A who?"

"Fashion designer."

"But that's jive," he blurted. "You going to college just to became some damn fashion designer?"

"May I ask what's wrong with that?"

"Everything." He wasn't putting her on now. He was disappointed. With all that big, intelligent talk, acting big, he expected her to want to be something —a doctor, a lawyer, a scientist. But messing around with clothes! "Hell, anybody can be that."

"I don't know about that!"

"Gail"—Ann Aimsley interrupted—"I think you'd better go out and get Perk. Your father will be home soon and you know how angry he gets when you girls are late."

"Maybe she stopped at Aunt Dora's." Imamu knew Gail wanted to keep sitting there to challenge him.

"Call and find out." Her mother was insistent. Annoyed, Gail hesitated before getting up and going out.

"And you"—Ann Aimsley handed Imamu a tablecloth—"can help me set the table."

There was more to setting a table than Imamu had imagined. Ann Aimsley gave instructions. "Knives and spoons go to your right, forks and napkins to your left." She put dishes down in the center of the table. "Bread and butter plates go to the left—" Imamu fumbled along as best he could.

"Mother, no one is home at Aunt Dora's," Gail said, coming back into the kitchen.

"Then go to Babs's," her mother said. "I keep telling her to come home first—"

Gail stood at the door, looking at Imamu, her expression reflecting her desire to keep their talk going. Imamu wanted her to stay. The spirit of their talk had gotten to him. He liked the feel of her across the table from him, the look in her round eyes, the anger in the heave of her chest. He wanted to shout at her and laugh with her, or at her, to feel her react to him, against him, and to let her know, "Baby, I might be the street but I ain't dumb."

"Do you want to walk with me, Imamu?" Gail asked. "Babs lives a few houses down the block."

"No," Ann Aimsley said. "Just go on so you can come back." Gail stalked out angrily.

Missing her the moment she left, Imamu asked, to hide his feelings, "Which are the bread and butter plates?"

Ann Aimsley picked up the small plate to show him. "The large plates go in the center," she said. "And the glasses—" She went to the glass cabinet and stood looking up.

Imamu got busy placing the dishes, forcing his eyes away from her and the glass cabinet. But her long silence troubled him, and when he heard her very softly, "Hello . . ." he stole a look at her, his heart sliding around in his chest. Seconds ticked away; finally he turned to face her.

But Ann Aimsley wasn't looking up at the top shelf. She was looking at the bottom shelf. "This looks like blood," she said. Then she studied the shelves. Imamu looked up to the top shelf. No, there was no way of telling, just by looking, that the glass was missing. He circled and recircled the table, arranging and rearranging things.

Then, unnerved by her silence, he took a chance and asked, "Where did you say the glasses went, Mrs. Aimsley?"

"Oh, yes." She took down five of the plain glasses from a lower shelf and handed them to him. "Above the knives," she said. Then she went to check the roast in the oven.

"The family is home!" The shout came from upstairs, followed by the sound of heavy footsteps thudding down the stairs. "The family is home. I smell it, I smell it." Peter Aimsley came through the door, a wide smile broadening through the grime and oil over his face. "That's the way a man's house should smell when he comes from work." He kissed his wife and winked at Imamu. "See what I mean, man? A happy home make a happy man. Where the girls? Upstairs?"

Ann Aimsley made a deliberately vague sound in her throat. "Hurry and get washed. Dinner is almost ready." And as her husband went upstairs, she shook her head. "Now why don't they come? The minute I work out peace in one department, something disturbs it in another." She started tossing the salad.

When Peter Aimsley came down he looked fresh and young in an open-neck sport shirt. He took his seat in front of the leg of lamb. "Where the girls?" he asked again as he took up the carving knife and fork. "They ain't upstairs."

"They should be in directly." Ann Aimsley got busy fussing around the kitchen.

"You come and sit down," Peter Aimsley said. "They know they should be home. I ain't waiting." The knife sliced through the meat with a burst of juice. The smile on his face said that it took more than absent daughters to kill the joy out of that. Imamu waited hungrily.

Peter Aimsley laid the first few slices of meat on Imamu's plate. Imamu helped himself to baked macaroni, candied sweet potatoes, and collard greens. When Ann Aimsley put the hot biscuits on the table, he grabbed for them. It wasn't real. Did folks eat like this every day?

The kitchen grew more and more quiet as they ate. Imamu cut off thinking. Once upon a time he had to have eaten like this. But that was long in the past. Nothing in his recent memory compared to this.

When he had almost finished with his first helping, he heard Peter Aimsley say, "No sense in punishing yourself because those two ain't got sense enough to know what they missing. Let them eat theirs cold." He pointed his knife at Imamu. "See what I mean? One somebody messes up and it messes with everything. Everybody." He kept right on eating. Imamu reached for seconds.

"I am a little worried," Ann Aimsley said. "Perk didn't come home from school. I sent Gail out to look for her. Why should they take all this time? Maybe Perk is somewhere hurt."

Peter Aimsley pointed his knife toward his wife. "Ain't nothing wrong with Perk except that she's spoiled. Like to do what she want."

"I don't spoil her by myself. You have more than a share in that yourself."

"Why, me?"

"Yes, you and her godmother—"

"Okay, then I won't spoil her any more. But when I give her my kind of punishment, I don't want you butting in—"

"Do I ever—"

Footsteps on the stairs made them stop their argument. They all looked toward the door. Gail came in, alone. "Mother, I have been all over. I even went to Aunt Dora. She wasn't home. I went to Babs. She hasn't even seen Perk. Mother, Perk didn't go to school at all today!"

10

"We been to all of Perk's other friends, Helen."
Peter was pleading with Babs's mother. "She's not
with them. Now you know Babs is her best friend.
So I'm asking you to let's look around in here
again." Imamu didn't understand why Peter Aimsley insisted Perk was at this particular house. It
made no kind of sense. Little Babs kept looking at
them and shaking her head.

"I swear, Mr. Aimsley," she said, "I didn't see
Perk all day. She didn't come by this morning. And
she didn't go to school. I swear."

"Peter," Babs's mother said, "we looked. I looked
even after you left the last time. There is no other
place in this house to hide. And I'm willing to
swear that Babs did not see Perk today."

Imamu leaned against the stoop, waiting. But
Peter Aimsley did not try to enter the house. "Okay,

Helen," he said after a while. "I'll stop bothering you. But see what you can get out of Babs."

"Babs don't know any more than she has already told. But I'll ask her again."

"Yeah, kids ain't nothing but a bunch of secrets."

"Whatever I find out I'll let you know. . . ."

Imamu followed Peter Aimsley back to the car and waited silently until he had started it and was driving away. Remembering how affectionate they were to each other, he was sure that wherever Dora Belle was, that's where they'd find Perk. Perhaps Peter thought so, too. They had already gone by Dora Belle's three times. She had not been home. So Imamu supposed that Peter Aimsley just wanted to kill some minutes before checking her out again.

"Girls." Peter Aimsley scoffed as though in answer to Imamu's unasked question. "Man don't know what they likely to do. Now take a boy. He stays out late and you can bet on him doing something he ain't got business to. You can just go up side of his head and ask questions later. Girls, no." He fell silent as he swung into a busy street and maneuvered the car through the traffic.

Imamu looked at the man's hands on the wheel of the car and remembered how he had been shaking, the night before, from fear they might go up side of *his* head. So although he didn't agree that girls were more twisted upstairs than dudes, he kept quiet. His feeling was that a dude might be out there thinking up a million things to do just to be doing something—or he might just get sucked into something, like he had with Iggy. Girls, now —most they were into was how to get next to a dude. Which, he was sure, was not what Perk was about.

"Take Gail," Peter Aimsley went on. "One time we had the police, the firemen, the whole neighborhood looking for her. She didn't show until the next day. The next day! Twenty-four hours later! And why? She just took it in her head to stay out. Liked to worry us to death. Know where she was? At one of her lil friends' house. We went there looking, man. Three times! Each time that lil girl swore out she hadn't seen Gail. Lied!"

Imamu liked the sound of Peter Aimsley's loud, almost angry voice. He liked the look of his hands on the wheel. He appreciated the buddy-to-buddy feeling that the man was trying for. For all of those reasons he didn't argue with his foster father. But he kept thinking of Perk waking him up that morning to button her dress. He remembered her impish grin and felt the need in her to win him over. To her he was still new. She had made up her mind to put him on her string of forever hers. She was that kind of little girl, he figured. So she wasn't about to stay with friends during his first week.

"That's why I keep backtracking," Peter Aimsley was saying. "That's why I make these mothers search their place, the closets. That's where Gail was hiding. Can you tie that one?" Peter Aimsley said in a fond voice. "And I bet you any money that's where we'll find Perk."

"I'd quicker think that Perk's with Dora Belle." Imamu let the thought ooze out. No, Perk would not be hiding. She had to be somewhere where she could show off. Because in that yellow dress, Perk was ready to party.

"Sure it ain't because you want to lay in on that buxom beauty?" Peter Aimsley nudged him with his elbow suggestively. "'BBB, that's my name for Dora Belle. Beautiful Buxom Beauty. She's my gal. Known her a long time. Matter of fact, she had me hooked first. But then she had enough of me and passed me on to her friend."

"Still go for her?" Imamu was surprised to hear himself asking.

"Who, me? Naw. Too proud. That's the reason Dora Belle ain't never married. She never thought that anyone was good enough for her. That was one beaut-i-ful wo-man." Peter Aimsley laughed. "She decided long ago to make it pay—hell, that's all she had. Although one time, she flipped out over my best buddy." He thought for a long time into the darkness, then laughed again. "Naw, I got myself the greatest woman living. Ann—she do a lot of things and think after, but I'll tell you one thing. She never stops going, never stops growing. Got to value a woman like that.

"But you watch out. Dora Belle's a lot of woman for a young stud like you." He laughed. Imamu blushed. It embarrassed him that Peter Aimsley should talk to him about women. He liked the idea, but it still embarrassed him.

They drove up one street and down another for a time before Imamu said, "Dora Belle asked me to give her a hand with her houses."

"Say how much she'd pay?"

"No, she left it up to me."

"Don't trust it. Make her name a price and then don't take the first five offers. She don't mean to be tricky—that's just part of that pride thing. She likes to think that she can have her way." He nudged Imamu again. "But what you need to hang around somebody's house for? You got yourself a home now."

Imamu looked into the car mirror and saw Peter Aimsley's warm look. The warmth flowed quickly through him. It embarrassed them both. Peter Aimsley looked away. "Yes, sir," he said. "I was a kid, no more than sixteen, when I started working to own my own. Worked in that same place—hard. Learned all there was to know about cars. Didn't need no schooling for that. Then I went to sea— merchant seaman. Came back, bought the sucker out. That's right. Never found me hanging on no street corners. I worked."

"Can I come to your place to work?" Imamu asked.

"Know anything about cars?"

"Naw."

"Too bad. Ain't got no time to be teaching. Busy."

Imamu wanted to remind Peter Aimsley that someone had to have taught him. He just didn't go into the shop knowing. But he drew back. He didn't want to mess with the feeling happening between them.

"Anyway," Peter Aimsley said, "you'll be starting back to school." It seemed that was the only talk that family was comfortable with: school. They probably had talked about his going long before he had gotten there.

"Maybe in the fall," Imamu said.

"Fall! You kidding? Don't tell me they ain't got summer schools." Imamu didn't answer. Even if he went to school in the fall it would be because he had done a whole summer's thinking on it. "Because I tell you, Imamu—that what they call you, Imamu?"

"Yes, sir."

"I tell you, Imamu, a boy needs school today more than they did in my day. So if they ain't got no summer schools in operation, we gonna build one for you. You a smart boy. Seen that right away. Ain't no sense in starting on cars. Hell, if you got to service some thing, service them space stations. See what I mean?"

Imamu squirmed. What was the matter with these old dudes? They stretched so far ahead of you, they didn't even see the ground they were stretching from. "Yeah, I getcha," he said, pretending to agree. "But I need a bit of change to hold in my pockets. Thought this summer I'd work awhile—"

"Sure, sure," Peter Aimsley said. They both were sliding gently around that warm feeling, wanting to hold on to it. "Good idea. Ain't nothing wrong with going to school a little, working a little. Only thing you don't need is some woman working you to death. That's what old Dora Belle will do for you—in more ways than one. Hah." He nudged Imamu in the ribs again. "Ain't nothing wrong in going by, giving her a hand now and then—mostly then. But every day? No man. Talk about pretty. That Dora Belle is pretty—pretty chinchy. Cheap as hell. She'd work you and expect you to pay."

He turned into Dora Belle's block. "Course, as young and pretty as you are, she likely will tie you into one of them houses. Ain't nothing wrong with that. Hell, I got my first experience with an older woman. But man, they drain you. Drain your ambition. And when they put you out, you know, they don't pay no alimony." He laughed. "Don't make sense starting out without ambition and without money, too. Get what I mean?"

Dora Belle was getting out of her car when they pulled up in front of her house. Peter Aimsley called to her out of the car window. "Where you been, lady? We been looking for you."

"Oh, Peter, is you? I been in town. Spent the day trying to get workmen to come for the house. I ain't get nobody."

"Where's Perk? She went with you?"

"Perk? How you mean? What Perk doing with me?"

"You ain't seen her?"

"It eleven o'clock in the night, Peter."

"So, she wasn't with you?"

"No, I tell you. I ain't see she the whole day."

Imamu's hopes stumbled, fell. If Perk wasn't with Dora Belle, she was nowhere. Of course he didn't actually *know*. He didn't know *them*. Hadn't been around long enough to tell. Yet he had a strange sinking feeling. He looked at Peter Aimsley, saw him looking suddenly lonely, unsure of himself. Imamu wanted to slap him on the shoulder, say, "Look, man, I'm here, you know. I'm here." But the eye with the cast in it looked past his face. In it was the hope. "Then she must have got home by now. Let's get home, Imamu. Let's go."

11

The two plainclothesmen were remarkable in how different they looked. They were both around six feet tall, but Sullivan had thinning black hair and ruddy skin. Age had added thickness rather than fat to his big frame. Otis Brown was younger and sported a high Afro and a heavy mustache. The brown skin was drawn tightly over his round face, and his bulging midsection obviously came from good living.

They were different in style, too. Sullivan had a studied carelessness and ruthless gray eyes. The clothes he wore—the dark blue suit with unpressed creases, the dark tie, the light blue shirt—seemed like a police uniform in which he took pride. His shoes were slightly scuffed, slightly run down. He was a working man, unconcerned with people's opinions of him. The creases of Brown's dark brown pants, on the other hand—keeping style with the brothers—were sharp enough to threaten any bend of his knees. The brown tweed sport jacket, the yellow shirt, the brown tie interwoven with golden threads, the shoes with the bought-today shine shouted to be taken for big time.

But around their eyes, they were the same—cops.

Imamu knew both well. He was born knowing them. He had played cops-and-black-boy games all his life. Their eyes said they'd take a dude apart —particularly if that dude happened to be black or Puerto Rican—for the "truth." The truth meant promotions. And they really earned those promotions in the black and Puerto Rican parts of the city. White cops like Sullivan could get a young black or Puerto Rican cat suffering from diarrhea of the mouth, or dead, in half an hour. It took black cats like Brown twenty-nine minutes; they had more to prove.

The two filled the Aimsley house. They crowded the floors, pushed out the walls of the living room, the kitchen. They had been called in to help. They ended up taking over.

Sullivan got up off his knees near the kitchen sink, and stood looking down at the Aimsleys. "Someone did bleed here," he said. "But not enough to suggest foul play."

"What else can it be?" Ann Aimsley's voice rose hysterically. "It can't be coincidence. I refuse to accept that it is coincidence—Perk missing—and then this blood."

Imamu found himself wishing that she had

changed from her house dress back to her skirt and blouse to speak to the policemen. That would have impressed them, made them look up to her. Instead they looked down. Her authority seemed as faded as the cotton dress she wore. And when Peter Aimsley put his arm around his wife in support, they both looked small—two ordinary people standing in the shadows of big men. Before they had seemed to Imamu so great.

That confused him. Their shrinking size, their diminishing importance. And as Mrs. Aimsley's hysteria grew, so did his confusion. He wanted to shout down her fears, wanted to say, "Wait up. That's my blood. I broke a glass. One of your expensive crystal glasses." Hell, a glass had to be worth a million dollars to bring about that mistake.

Imamu turned to Dora Belle, expecting her to speak, tell them that he had cut himself and had gone to her. But Dora Belle was looking at him, questioning him with her eyes, demanding that he speak for himself. Imamu turned again to Mrs. Aimsley, opened his mouth, closed it. Weird. He had never called her "Mother." But to call her Mrs. Aimsley in front of these policemen had to draw their attention to the fact that he did not belong to the house.

Sullivan, always on the lookout for signs, caught his hesitation. The big man cold-stared him. Imamu stared back unblinking, his back arching. Sullivan's eyes snapped wise—street wise. They had recognized each other.

Turning from Imamu, Sullivan studied the others in the kitchen. He stared hard at Dora Belle, who returned his stare with a brazen, prideful one of her own. His eyes went to Mr. and Mrs. Aimsley, encircled by their home, their quality furnishings. He looked at Gail, tall, precious, pointedly alert. Then he signaled his partner with a slight jerk of his head.

"What's he doing here?" he asked the Aimsleys.

"I live here," Imamu cried out before anyone else could answer.

"Yeah?" Sullivan deliberately turned his back on Imamu. "How long has he been here?"

Again Imamu answered. "What's it to you?"

"I want to know." Sullivan kept talking to the Aimsleys.

"Ain't none of your business," Imamu snapped.

"I'm making it my business, punk."

"Two days," Ann Aimsley answered, her voice quivering. "Only two days."

"Only two days, huh?" The gray eyes studied Imamu coldly. "Where's his room?"

"Upstairs," Ann Aimsley said.

"Mind showing it to me?"

The two of them left the kitchen to go upstairs. And those left in the kitchen kept their eyes busy so they would not look at Imamu. Sensing this, Imamu felt betrayed. Ann Aimsley had gone upstairs with Detective Sullivan to sell him out. He tried to push the thought aside but it remained. It grew. And then they were coming back into the kitchen. "This yours?" Sullivan asked Imamu.

Imamu stared at the yellow satin ribbon that Perk had dropped in his room that morning. "Mind telling me how this got in your room?" Sullivan's hard eyes bored through Imamu's. Imamu looked from him to Ann Aimsley. He saw fear beating like a pulse in her eyes. Why? What did she think he had done to Perk? His scalp crawled, his ears burned. Betrayed, betrayed.

"I don't have to answer you." He turned to Sullivan. "I know my rights."

"Well now, what you need rights for?"

"To deal with mothers—like you." He kept his eyes from Ann Aimsley as he spoke.

"I didn't accuse you of nothing—yet."

"I ain't done nothing. I can prove I ain't done nothing."

Imamu heard his words tumbling out. He tried to stop them. Tried to change the guilty sound of them. He couldn't. They seemed to play through him as if he were a record and the cops had put a needle on him. He had used those same words before. He always used them. His friends on the block used them. His Legal Aid lawyers used them. They were his words, words for people like him. "I know my rights. . . ."

He felt a drawing-away from him. Without looking he saw them: Dora Belle with her puzzled look, Ann Aimsley, her eyes going mad with fear (why hadn't she put on a skirt with a classy blouse?), Peter Aimsley, his wandering eye shocked into space, Gail—Gail? He longed to look at her, see what she thought. For two days, he had been on the receiving end of words; now he was saying them. Couldn't stop himself.

"What happened to your hand?" Sullivan asked.

"Ain't nothing to do with you."

"I'm asking you a question. Don't let me get mean."

"And I say it ain't got nothing to do with you."

"He hurt his hand at my Aunt Dora's," Gail said.

"Nuh, man," Dora Belle said. "He come to me with he cut hand. I bandage it."

"You lied! You lied!" Ann Aimsley screeched at Imamu.

Imamu kept his eyes on Sullivan.

"He cut he hand on one of Ann's crystal glass," Dora Belle explained. "Is he blood you must see there." She got up, and going to the glass cabinet, opened it and looked up at the top shelf. "Eh-eh," she cried. "But they look all there."

Heads turned toward the glass cabinet. Eyes stared up, following Dora Belle's. Crazy! All they had to do was count them! He wanted to laugh. Everything was so simple. But if it was so simple, why didn't *he* tell them to count them? And then he heard Ann Aimsley's voice, shouting, accusing. "What did you do with her? What did you do with my child!"

Imamu stared at her. She was speaking to him! Impossible. She was scared for Perk, but she was still in his corner! What was she saying? Did she know what she was doing? Good, kind, gentle, intelligent woman. Did she know what she was doing? She knew that everything about him had to be clean. Hadn't she come into court to listen, to make sure the law had seen about his rights? So why was she throwing him to the law now? He trusted her. Dug her.

"Okay, Okay, out with it. What did you do with the kid?" Otis Brown shouldered Sullivan aside. Imamu's senses shifted with the shift of authority, but his eyes stayed on Ann Aimsley. He heard the new harshness, knew that this was the moment that Brown had been preening for. He had to show his stuff, in front of Gail, but more, in front of his white partner. Imamu knew it but he couldn't take his eyes from Ann Aimsley's half-crazed face.

"Hear me? I'm talking to you, man. What you do with her?"

Imamu heard. Knew that rights talk didn't make it with the Browns. They both knew about rights. What was happening was all about Brown's making it. About Brown showing that he knew more about *his* people, that he could squeeze what he wanted out of his people. While it was true that Sullivan might get more promotions, he, Brown, was the one who merited them with his special skills. He knew best how to soften the heads of niggers. Imamu knew it all. He felt it in the strong body standing over him, intimidating him with the smell of death. But he could not shift his eyes away from Ann Aimsley's staring, accusing gaze.

"I'm asking you just one more time." Brown's fingers pushed at Imamu's shoulder until he forced

Imamu to look at him. Imamu gave it to him right in his blackness in front of his white partner.

"You a simple mother, man."

Brown's eyes narrowed, his mustache quivered. Sullivan took over. "You didn't answer about your hand," he said softly.

Crazy things were happening to Imamu, inside of him. Sure he could say that he had cut himself. Make someone climb the chair and count the glasses. Count them himself. But he didn't dig Sullivan acting so wise about him and Brown. Thinking *he knew them*. Using their natural dislike for each other to keep his promotions going. And for Imamu, beneath it all there was a getting-even, a feeling of spite directed at the hysterical Ann Aimsley.

Let her suffer. Let her think that he did something to Perk, that she had brought him into her home and he had kicked her in the face in return. Yes, things were happening to him, in him. Deep. He shook his head and laughed, laughed in his throat.

"We can take you where we can make you talk," Brown said.

Imamu looked at Peter Aimsley to see his reaction. But Peter Aimsley's wandering eye went past his shoulder. He didn't want to look at him. Yeah, those few moments they had spent together in the car had trapped him, too, had made him want to believe in him. They had felt something out there; now he didn't know. His wife had brought Imamu into the house against his wishes. She had turned against him. Peter Aimsley didn't know.

"Where do you think that will get you?" Imamu spoke into Brown's waiting face.

"I'll tell you where." Brown grabbed Imamu's arm. "Just as far as we can make you go."

12

Things had happened so quickly that after the police led Imamu away, Gail's mind was as blank as the night outside the window. Then the events of the evening strung themselves through her mind like a moving picture. Remembering the last few moments, she felt ashamed. She looked at her mother, still hysterical, crying, in her father's arms, at her father holding her mother as though that might be an answer to Perk's not being there. She saw Dora Belle at the table, staring in a kind of confusion, a numbness that was far from her usual quick-witted self. She saw herself as though from afar, numb, unable to give meaning to what had happened, was happening.

Perk had gone out this morning and had not come back. Had something terrible happened to her? Or had she been taken by some devilish whim and gone off somewhere, to come back tomorrow?

What if she had? Then how could any one of them face Imamu?

Her face burned as she remembered thinking, at first, that he had been in some way responsible for Perk's disappearance. Why had their lives changed just forty-eight hours after he had walked into their house and into their lives, she had asked herself. Tall, arrogant, silent, he brought in with him the uneasiness of the street, a ready-made answer.

She listened to her mother's sobs, the self-pitying wail. "It's my fault. It's my fault." Gail sought her father's eyes. He was looking toward the door through which the detectives had pushed Imamu. He kept brushing his wife's hair, trying to console her, but there was confusion, doubt in his look. No, he didn't believe Imamu was guilty.

"To think that I brought him into this house," Ann Aimsley whimpered. "That criminal—into our home."

"Mother!" Gail cried. Then, as the whimpering kept on, she said, "We are the ones who are the criminals!"

"We?" Her father turned to her as though he expected her to have all the answers.

"Yes, we! But you, Mother, more than any of us!"

"Gail!" the three adults shouted together. It was as though because they had known each other for so long, their reactions were timed to be the same.

"You were afraid of him!" Gail said. "From the first!" She felt the hysteria in the room enter her. She tried to struggle against it, tried to calm herself, but she heard herself hitting out. "Yes, you

were afraid of him! But you brought him home!
You didn't care what anybody said!"

"Don't talk to your mother like that!" Peter
Aimsley shouted.

"You just wanted to feel important." Gail kept
at her mother.

"I won't have it!" Peter Aimsley roared. "Do you
hear? I won't have it!"

"My child. I want my child back," Ann Aimsley
screamed.

"But how could you do it?" Gail's voice kept
rising. "How could you bring Imamu here and then
condemn him!"

"He condemned himself!" Peter Aimsley shouted.
"He ain't had to break bad with them. Why ain't
he answered what they ask?"

"He's innocent!" Gail screamed. For suddenly
the one thing in the entire evening which made
sense was the pain in Imamu's face when he had
looked at her mother. It was a pain so complete, so
sharp that it had shafted her, pinning her to him
with her faith. "Mother, he trusted you!"

"You care more about them little things like
trust than you care about your own sister!" her
father said. The doubt about Imamu's guilt was
gone from his eyes.

"You can't say that to me!" Gail shrieked. "You
must know I care. I care more than anything in the
world! What good will it do Perk for the police to
hold Imamu."

"They'll squeeze something out of him!" Peter
Aimsley kept shouting.

"You believe that! You believe that!"

"Yes. I'll kill him. You hear me! I'll kill him!"

"Perk. Perk. Perk." Dora Belle screamed. "Oh God, oh God, oh God. I ain't want to think a she out there by sheself. I did hold she in me arms . . ."

"Stop that!" Peter Aimsley turned on Dora Belle. "Don't cry unless you got reason. And you ain't got reason, understand!"

But Dora Belle kept screeching. "She like me own. Me own. Me own." She rocked herself back and forth.

"I said stop it! Do you hear!" Dora Belle held on to her tears and for a few minutes, the deep breathing of blocked emotions brought back a certain calm.

"And that poor Imamu," Dora Belle muttered, tears running down her cheeks.

"You, too?" Ann Aimsley whispered. "You, too?"

"I ain't know he do nothing," Dora Belle whispered in her turn. "He cut he hand. He came to me house. I fix it."

"Then why did you say he lied?" Gail asked.

"Who, me? Not me. I say your mother crystal ain't break. That's all. He tell me he get cut with your mother crystal glass—"

"Then that's his blood," Gail said.

"No, it's Perk's blood." Ann Aimsley's cry rose again.

"If Imamu cut himself, then it's his blood." Gail stared at the woman, who seemed to be melting under her eye. "And if he said he did it with a crystal glass, it's a crystal glass he cut himself with!"

She walked to the sink and looked around. From experience she knew how impossible it was to pick up every piece of broken glass. Imamu had tried to wipe up his blood and had not succeeded. It was much easier to wipe up blood than to sweep shattered glass. Almost immediately she saw some slivers wedged in the crack between the linoleum and the base of the sink. She picked them up and put them on the table.

"That proves Imamu did break a glass," she said.

"It does no such thing," Ann Aimsley said. "Little pieces of glass could have been there forever."

Gail stared at her mother. She might have expected an answer like that from her father. But the way Ann Aimsley kept house . . .

"Why are you staring at me that way, Gail?"

"Did you ever break any of your crystal glasses, Mother?"

"What a question."

"Did you?"

"No."

Gail took a chair to the cabinet, and standing on it counted the crystal glasses, banging them together with a carelessness that ordinarily would have pained Ann Aimsley. There were sixteen of each—highball, martini, whisky, water—but of the wine glasses there were only fifteen.

"Then the boy ain't lie," Dora Belle said, looking from Ann to Peter Aimsley.

"Perk must have seen him when he broke it," Ann Aimsley said.

"And?" Gail was puzzled. "And what . . . "

"If all he did was break a glass, Gail, why didn't he tell me?"

"I guess for the same reason that I never tell you when I break a glass."

"What are you saying?"

"I break glasses all the time, Mother. So does Perk. But we keep them hidden until we can replace them. We know how you value things."

"Gail!" Ann Aimsley cried. But Peter Aimsley pointed his finger at Gail.

"Listen you, the care that your mother put in this house is what made a decent home to bring you up in. That came before college and all your big talk—"

"Stop, Peter, for God's sake." Ann Aimsley's voice broke again. "What are you accusing me of, Gail?"

"I don't know," Gail said. And she didn't. In wonder she had to admit that her mother's mind had twists and turns that she had never taken the time to follow. "I don't know," she repeated in surprise. "All I know is that I'm going to get Imamu out."

"Let him stay where he is." Peter Aimsley tried to take command.

"I will not! The least we can do is tell the police about the glass . . . show that we care."

"Care!" her father exploded. "One thing I care about, is Perk. Do you understand that? My little girl. Let the police find out . . ."

"I'm going," Gail said.

"It's after one . . ." Ann Aimsley said.

"And where will you take him?" her father asked. She stared at him, hard. He was no longer confused. Only angry.

"I don't care," Gail said. "I will not let him stay in jail!"

"If you go after him, just keep on going," Peter Aimsley said.

"I might just do that," Gail answered. "I might do just that."

"But what you quarreling?" Dora Belle asked. "If you ain't want the boy here, let he stay with me." The three Aimsleys turned and stared at her.

Detective Otis Brown pushed his face up to Imamu's and squinted his eyes. "Look, man," he said, "you gonna tell us what we want to know anyway, so why don't you just make it easy on yourself and talk now."

Imamu looked away from the eyes. Their lack of expression meant total evil to him. He stared into a corner of the square little room, trying to hold on to his anger, which at least made him feel equal to whatever they could give. But from the minute the door had closed them in, cutting them off from all contact with the rest of the police station, his anger had begun to be replaced by fear. It gushed out of his pores so, that he smelled it. Detective Otis Brown did, too.

The last time, in another precinct, in this same kind of windowless room, he had been able to hang on to his anger—act bad, let the cops do their worst. They had been evil suckers, too, yet he had been able to hold on. Imamu passed his tongue over dry lips. What was happening this time? Imamu reached into his pocket for a toothpick. Brown grabbed his hand. "What you got there?" He took the tooth-pick from Imamu and threw it to the floor. "And take them clothes off, anyway; you ain't gonna need them."

"Look, man . . ."

"You ain't got but a minute . . ."

Imamu felt his head grow cold. He knew what this meant. He had never gone through the cold towel and hose treatment before, but he knew all about it. Knew dudes who had gone through it. It was bad.

If only he had somebody pulling for him. The last time Iggy had been a room or so away. He had known that Iggy was in his corner. He might be a killer but he was his boy. It was hell having nobody.

Sitting naked in the straight-backed chair, he thought of Ann Aimsley. God, he had dug her. And she had thrown him to them. He tried to change his feeling for her to hate, but he had no hate to pull from. No anger, no hate, no support—only fear. It was his bare behind and these jokers. The chair he sat on rattled, and it was minutes before he realized that it was his shaking that rattled the chair.

"Look, man, I ain't done nothing," he said pleadingly. He hated his pleading. "I cut my hand. That's all." The difference in tone from the way he had been talking at the house got to him. But he kept on. "That was my blood, man . . ."

"How come you ain't said that before?" Brown grabbed his hand and snatched off the bandage. "Who you jiving?" he asked. "That cut ain't give that much blood. How'd it happen?"

"That lady told you. The glass. Why you all ain't look, man?"

"What about that ribbon? Guess that was yours—"

"I found it. Picked it up on the steps."

"Yeah, yeah, now let's talk about the little girl. You seen her?"

"I live in the house man. I got to have seen her."

"When did you see her last?"

"This morning."

"Before she was missing?"

"Got to be before she was missing, man." Simple questions thrown at you to trick you. "They all seen her before she was missing."

"You seen her leave the house?"

"Yeah—no. I ain't seen her leave. I was in bed."

"What you do when you get up?"

"Lots of things. Cooked breakfast, broke that glass . . ."

"That when she come back?"

"She ain't come back. I ain't seen her."

"I thought you said you seen her."

Sullivan coming back into the room interrupted the interrogation. "Yeah, Brown, we got a file on this boy. Long one. Petty theft, breaking and entering. The last one though is something: he and his boys offed a grocer—name of Fein."

Sullivan's face had changed—not much—just enough to give the message that the proving ground had nothing to do with a missing girl named Perk and everything to do with a dead dude named Fein.

"Don't say?" Brown spoke softly. His brown face shone with sweat. He had taken off his jacket; now he untied his tie. "So you beat a murder rap." Wrapping a handkerchief over his fist, he stood looking down at Imamu. "Guess that makes you go for slick." Imamu's head jerked back. He tasted blood. He looked up to see Brown readjusting the handkerchief.

"Hold it. Hold it." Sullivan handed Brown some wet towels. "My partner is impatient." He smiled a twisted smile. "Always in a hurry. Know you're glad I'm around."

Sullivan picked up the rubber hoses. They seemed to Imamu to be about six feet long, but they were maybe three feet. One for Sullivan and one for Brown. Seeing the hoses, he broke out in sweat despite the cold towels draped around him. In a panic he scraped his mind for words—begging words, praying words, confession . . . it didn't matter what he confessed to. Talk now. Change later. Then he looked into their faces and he knew it didn't matter. It was no use. Their eyes reminded him of Iggy's. Both of them! Nothing he confessed would change their minds. They got their kicks from kicking asses, from killing—like Iggy. Yeah, there were dudes like Iggy and there were dudes like these two. And all in between were guys like him, like Fein—the victims. That's what it was all about.

And seeing this, Imamu gave up. Only they didn't know that he had given up. "Okay." Sullivan grinned. "Now what is this you were telling us about rights?" He rushed at Imamu, his hand raised, then brought the rubber hose down across Imamu's arm. The arm went limp. It fell to the side of the chair. Imamu left it there, weighted like death.

"Yeah, tell us about rights, man." Brown rushed him with his length of hose, came down on his other side. That hand fell to the side of the chair. Imamu curled up inside himself to look at them. He might die. That was the worst that could happen. He didn't mind. He chuckled to himself. Knowing that he was in the hands of cats like these and that there was nothing he could do made it cool. They'd just shovel him out and shovel another dude just like him in—into the same chair. The grand parade.

Imamu thought of the young Puerto Rican boy in the other precinct who had been brought out of one of these rooms while Imamu was waiting. The boy's face had been smooth, like wax—beyond pain. His mother, though—she had cried. Screamed like it was she who had been beaten, was dying.

But no one would come for him. No one would come to cry or scream or care, even if he was dead. What kind of holes did they throw dudes like him in? Or did they take their bodies to labs for experiments? It didn't matter. He thought of Ann Aimsley, of his mother. Tried to get mad, think up hate. Didn't work. He had to be a weird dude not to hate those responsible for his death.

"Go back to Brooklyn," his mother had advised. And he had gone. And so Ann Aimsley had handed him here, with love. He chuckled silently as he felt his body shake from the force of another blow. And so he'd never see either one of them again. He didn't give a damn. People hurt too much when you gave a damn. He thought of Dora Belle. Looka here what I missed out on. That deserved a long laugh. And he chuckled inside himself. Pretty lady, all those pretty clothes, pretty hair, and three houses! Goddamn. Three houses and I'm missing out. He wanted to laugh out loud. Then he thought about Perk.

Perky Perk. He felt her warmth. Her round, warm body as she pushed him awake. God, he wished he had grabbed her, hugged her, felt her warm beside him, cuddly and cute. She was okay. No phoney. Straight. Talked a lot to get him mad. But being mad at her only meant he had to get glad, get over being mad with her. That was her strength over people, over him. She had wanted him enough to have made him mad. She had to know if she had made him glad. That's how he knew she wasn't ever coming back. If she had been able, Perk would have rushed home from her school party to see where she stood with him.

Funny, thought, if she did get back. Damn funny

if she had just gone to sleep at one of her little friends and came back home after he was dead. Ha-ha. Then he got serious inside, all the way deep inside. No, Perk hadn't gone to sleep with any friend. She was gone! Somebody out there had done something to her. And now, he'd never know. They'd never know. With him dead they'd believe that everything he knew about her died with him and was buried with him. And thinking that, Imamu's need to live stirred. He didn't want to die. He had to know what had happened to Perk.

Sullivan's voice came through to Imamu as though from a long distance: "This is one tough nigger. He's taking a long time to break. What say boy, how is it you killed a white man and beat the rap?"

Brown's voice came next. "All I want to know, man, is what done happened to a lil black gal. That's what he's here for—know what I mean?"

Imamu wanted to laugh loud. They'd never solve that one, either. That duel would keep up between them for life. But thinking of Perk had made his mind spring back to life. That was how he happened to see Brown reach into a corner and take out a black-handled hatchet with a four-inch-long gleaming blade.

"Now," Brown said, as he tested its edges. "We giving you one more chance. You talk or that's it, baby. Giving you three."

These cats were really crazy! It was one thing for him to die and for them to say he had died of an overdose or some such thing. Another, for them to send his head one place and his body another, when folks knew he had come here in one piece. What kind of excuse could they think up?

"One ... two ... three!" The hatchet descended. Imamu jerked his head aside, screaming out in terror: "Mama!" It hit his neck. He saw the blood spilling out everywhere, down the white towels, on to his legs. For one instant, he saw himself stepping into the Aimsley living room. He stared around confused at the dustfree tables; he saw the painting of the sea, the forceful wave breaking over his eyes.

He turned his head slowly and looked into Brown's narrowed eyes. He moved to look into Sullivan's cold gray eyes. He had turned his head! A familiar smell, the sweet sticky smell of tomato ketchup, rose to sting his nostrils. A trick. A goddamn fool trick!

"That," said Brown, looking down at him from a great height, "was only a test. The next time, it will be for real."

But with his relief, Imamu's bowels loosened. Sullivan turned squeamish. "That tough nigger's just messed all over himself. Get him outa here. Get him the hell on outa here."

13

Gail had expected the police station to be filled with characters from the underbelly of the city, ogres of the night who did battle with an army of policemen and were carted off, humbled or bloody, to fill the city's jails while the rest of the city slept. She had supposed that she would be crushed among them in the same way that she was crushed on the subway during rush hour. But the station was quiet, presided over by an elderly uniformed officer who sat at his desk, looking over official papers. Only two people were waiting in the hall-like chamber. One was a drunk black woman sitting at the other end of the bench, who would wake intermittently to swear in a loud, hoarse whisper. The other was a short white man dressed in black, who walked aimlessly from one side of the room to the other.

Only occasionally did a few tired-looking policemen come in with prisoners—mostly young men, handcuffed. They would stop at the desk to give or exchange information with the officer, then disappear through a side door, reappearing minutes later, having disposed of their burdens on the other side of the door.

At one point the drunken woman looked over at Gail and muttered, "No good— No damn good— Keep in some damn trouble—" Then she drifted off to sleep again. Gail turned her head away and tried to squeeze herself as thin as a pencil, hoping to lengthen the distance between them. She wanted to change her seat, get away from the foul smell of stale alcohol. But she was unwilling to let the two white men get the idea that she might be putting down a black woman just because she was drunk. On the other hand, she didn't want the woman to think that she had common cause with her just because she was black.

After what seemed to be hours, a policeman came out of the side door, followed by a white youth. "Mr. Vincent?" the officer at the desk called. But the man dressed in black had already gone to stand at the side of the boy and had put his arm around his shoulders. The boy shrugged it off. "Here he is," the officer said. "Free, this time. But don't make it a habit. I don't want to see you back here again." The boy walked out, not seeming to hear the warning. His father trailed behind. The officer went back to his papers.

Gail stared at the elderly man behind the desk, wondering if anything ever troubled him. She had come in, asked for Imamu. He had simply said, "Yeah? Sit down."

"But I want to explain," she had said. "You see he didn't lie about the glass—" She hadn't known what else to add; Imamu had not come in because he had broken a glass. But the indifferent officer had merely said, "I know. Sit down." And she had sat.

Gail eased back on the bench wondering if he remembered that she was there. The only reason he had let her stay was because they were releasing Imamu. Someone—Dora Belle, her mother, or maybe even her father—must have called to tell them about the glass. Or why were they releasing him? Why would he let her sit?

She was tired, very tired. Never before had she passed an entire night without sleep. And as the gray of the morning gave way to pink, she wanted to rest her head, close her eyes. Instead she sat straight-back and alert, afraid that she might fall asleep. They had come to a busy hour. Many more policemen came in with prisoners. People came in with complaints; some seemed worn out from not having slept, others from just having awakened. In a short time—a few hours—the entire world would be awake. Sleepy faces would brighten over coffee into eager faces intent on being first, on subways, buses, jobs. She ought to be a part of that day. But she still hung on to yesterday. Perk was a part of yesterday. And today? Strange, not even twenty-four hours had passed, and somehow the family seemed to have come to the end of a strange and tragic road.

Which way were they going to turn? What action could they take? Were they only to sit and wait? At home? The same way she was waiting here? They would all die! Who would help them? Imamu? Somehow she didn't see him waiting—letting them all die.

And as she thought of him, he walked through the door. Gail's heartbeat quickened. And then she knew why she had sounded so confused, that day with Celia, why she had felt so annoyed from the moment he had walked into their house. She knew that she didn't want a time when she didn't expect him to walk into a place where she was waiting. And as she got up to go to him something in her shouted: But we are so young!

She studied him silently as he slouched over, his hands in his pockets. He must be tired. The night had been long for him, too. But with his hair bushed out neatly, his shirt open to the waist, the toothpick twisting about from one side of his mouth to the other, he might have just come from a walk around the block.

"Jones"—the officer called his name—"we don't have enough to hold you on. But if we get anything, look out." Then he went back to his papers. Routine.

"Imamu," Gail said, and when he turned to look at her, she noticed the thickness of his lips. He had been hit, beaten maybe, but the bruising was covered by his dark skin. And seeing him so calm, so cool, still arrogant, then remembering the pain she had witnessed in his eyes a few hours before, she wondered about black men and how much of their pain was hidden by their blackness.

"Imamu," she repeated. But there was no answering gladness when he turned to her, no recognition that they were meant to be together. He simply looked at her and looked away. "I came to get you, Imamu."

It didn't matter that she had nowhere to take him, that he wasn't even glad to see her. The important thing to her now was that she had come, that he knew he was not alone, that he never had to be alone. She believed in him. She cared.

His eyes left hers to drift over to the sleeping woman. They stayed on the woman as he asked, "Why?"

Crazy question. What crazy answer could she give: to be by your side? To walk the streets with you? To stay by your side until we find Perk? Until Perk comes home. He had to care about that. He had to care that she knew he had nothing to do with it.

"To take you home," she said. Was that a lie? No! Everyone had to see how important it was that he be home, that whatever they had to do, they had to do it with him. They had to find Perk together. They knew the police wouldn't find her. They knew, as she knew, as Imamu knew, that the police didn't care about finding a little black girl.

"Why?" he repeated. "She send you?"

A flush of resentment pushed through her as she

remembered the fight she had had with her parents, the hours she had spent waiting in the station. But more, she felt jealous that he thought more of her mother than he did of her.

"So she didn't send you," he said as though that was the important thing to him. Then he walked past her to go over to the sleeping woman.

"Ma." He shook her. "Come on, get up. I'm taking you home."

The woman looked up at him. "Oh, is you." Sitting up she tried to get to her feet, fell back. "Whatcha get them to drag me down here— Outa my bed—"

"Come on, let's go." He put his hand under her arm, pulled her up.

"Le's go— le's go," she said, mocking him. "Who they got you for killing this time?"

Imamu seemed not to hear. He held her steady, maneuvering her toward the door. "Ought to keep your butt—s'where you gonna end." She staggered against him drunkenly.

Gail followed them past the unseeing officer, out of the station. As they walked up the block panic replaced her resentment. It grew as they kept putting distance between themselves and the station. Quickening her steps, she followed them. "Don't go with her, Imamu," she cried. "You can't go with her. She hates you."

They kept on walking and Gail struggled to still her mounting terror at the sight of the tall, straight boy and the drunken woman going off together, but not belonging together. She wanted to grab hold of the woman, beat her off, beg Imamu to run, go as fast as he could, get away. But it was Imamu who held on to the woman, Imamu who refused to listen. In desperation, Gail, forgetting her indictment of the police a short time before, thought of running back to the station for help. She wanted to tell them that Imamu had no right being with his mother. That *her* mother had been appointed his guardian by the court. But she didn't want to go back. She might lose sight of them. She kept following them.

A car pulled alongside of her and someone called out, "Gail!"

"Mother!" Gail rushed to the car.

"I came to get you, Gail. There is no sense—"

"Mother, stop them," Gail cried, pointing in desperation to the pair who were turning the corner. "Imamu is going home with his mother! You can't let him!"

"Come on. Let's go home, Gail." Ann Aimsley opened the door of the car. "Your father is so upset—"

Gail ran to catch up with Imamu and his mother. She was determined that Imamu should not go off with her. She just hadn't thought of how to prevent them.

But her mother drove up to Imamu. Getting out of the car, she spoke to him. "Look, Imamu. I don't know—I can't think. I only know Gail has to come home. Her father's so upset . . ."

Imamu stared broodingly at her for a few seconds. "I'm not upset," he said.

"Of course you are. But look, Gail and her father quarreled. You must know that, at a time like this . . . look, I've just got to take Gail home."

"Take her." He shrugged.

"But I'm not going," Gail cried. "I'm not leaving Imamu." But Ann Aimsley kept talking to Imamu as though Gail's decision were up to him.

"Look, Imamu, Gail called me a criminal. I feel like one. Maybe I was wrong. But I can't think! Can you understand that? I can't think. You know I wanted you to be with us. Wanted to make a home for you. It's just that, right now, I can't think. Look, Imamu, let's give it time. Let's see what happens. . . . Maybe you do belong . . ."

Imamu laughed in his throat. He took out his toothpick and threw it away. Then, leveling his eyes at her, he said, "Don't make me no difference whether I belong or not." His soft voice had become harsh, threatening. "I'm coming back."

"You are what?" Ann Aimsley backed away from the threat in his voice.

"I'm coming back," he repeated, still staring into her eyes. "You see, Mrs. Aimsley, all night long I had to deal with folks messing in my head. Them bulls mess in my head last night. Maybe they ought to have killed me. You messed in my head. Now that was wrong. Ain't no sense in folks messing in other folks' heads, unless they willing to go all the way. See what I mean? You"—he pointed at her, so that she cringed against the car—"went all the way inside, took off a piece of my brain. Now you saying that you can't think. Lady, you outa your mind! Maybe we all outa our minds. What you think I'm about? You think I can stay in Harlem with a piece of my brain in Brooklyn? Not knowing what's happening? It just ain't gonna be that way—no way."

"What do you mean?" Ann Aimsley's voice was faint.

"Mother, what he's saying is that you accused him, and that he has no intentions of going to hang out in Harlem until he knows what's happened to Perk. Is that right, Imamu?"

"Ri-ght," Imamu answered. "Now unless you got something to add to that, I'm taking my old lady home." His mother had been leaning against a parked car. Now Imamu pulled her from it and tucked her arm through his. "See," he said to Ann Aimsley, "this here is a great lady. Great lady. She can't hardly walk, yet she made it all the way from Harlem to get me. The lady loves me." He walked away from them.

Gail watched them go. The terror over Imamu's welfare subsided. He had to take his mother home. He was that kind of person. Her heartbeat marked time to their footsteps as they walked away. But he was coming back. He had to. He had seen the same clear image drawn across his mind as she had. And like her, he knew that if Perk was to be found, they would find her together.

14

The two of them remained silent during the long subway ride up to Harlem—held that way in the pain of being together. His mother had escaped into sleep, while Imamu escaped only because weariness had knotted his brain, making it impossible to think.

But when they arrived at the old apartment, when it had closed in around them, their footsteps threading through the long shafts of dust in the hazy sunlight, his mother's fear came leaping out at him.

"No good— No damn good," she muttered drunkenly, and going directly to her room, she threw herself across the bed.

"Take your things off," he ordered, reaching for the black shawl around her shoulders. She snatched herself away, glaring at him.

"Don't touch me!" she cried out, twisting her head not to look at him. "Good as that woman been to you, you gone and mess up . . ." She let the shawl fall to the floor, and kicking off her worn shoes, settled down on the bed, her eyes closed.

Imamu stared down at her, waiting. When she didn't move he called, "Ma?"

She turned her back, repeating, "Gone and mess up . . ."

"Mess up? Mess up like how, Ma?"

"What you gone and done to that lil gal—"

Imamu waited for her to add: "Kill her too?" The unspoken words fanned silently between them brushing up their feelings toward each other. "Like what, Ma?"

But she wasn't able to deal with her words. All she wanted was for him to leave so she could hide herself inside herself. And even as he stood looking, her face slackened, the once firm mouth fell open. He shook her. "Ma . . ."

She turned on her back, looking all the way up, trying to focus. "Get away," she cried. "Go—go—go to a decent place . . ." She had given up to total fear—fear heaped upon fear. It was fear of him, fear of the neighborhood, fear of the neighbors' fears, fears of the neighbors' pain—she had built a mountain of fears up around her from which she had to hide.

Imamu could see the face of Ann Aimsley with her fear at his threat to return on it. He tried to cut it out of his mind, but the two images lingered, fused into one.

The minutes raced by, and as a snarl of snores rasped through his mother's throat, Imamu clenched his fists to keep himself from squeezing her face awake, beating on it, demanding of it: "What about me! I didn't born myself! I didn't put myself in this crap! I found myself here! Kill me! Kill me for surviving!"

His body shook with his need to pull her out of bed, drag her into the bathroom, push her face into the toilet bowl, and wash it there, force her to break down the mountain of fear and become responsible for what she said. But he shook his head. He wanted to want to do those things. He wanted to want her to face her fears, to believe him. But did he really care? He walked out of her bedroom and went into his. The night had been heavy. Too heavy, on all of him.

Dull from dirt on the window, the eerie sunlight distorted shapes, making craters in the disorder of the room. Imamu pushed aside the twisted sheets to make room for his body and dropped heavily onto his bed. He lay staring up at the ceiling for a while, and fell asleep at last.

When he awakened, he lay in darkness trying to remember. His body ached and held him to the bed. Closing his eyes, he flexed his muscles, one by one. Every one ached, every one was too heavy to move. Then two faces slipped into his mind and hovered behind his eyes: Brown. Sullivan. Imamu studied their faces. Their cold, unsaying eyes. Then he laughed in his throat. "Imamu, baby, you is one lucky black boy." There were two things a black dude off the streets could do nothing about: death and the po-lice. He chuckled. He had come out ahead. But a sudden rush of blood heated his face, followed by sweat: God, had Gail smelled anything?

Thinking of Gail made him remember. He was home. He tried lifting his arm to switch on the light over his bed. His arm didn't move. He lay quietly, letting events come back. He thought of the bed where he lay, the dirty sheets, the cracked walls of the room, of his dirty clothes still scattered over the room. "Man, I sure didn't lie down here to die!"

From habit he listened for sounds from his mother's room. What time was it, anyway? Had she gotten up? Gone out? Did it matter? The fused image of her face and Ann Aimsley's branded in the front of his brain forced him into some cold thinking.

A kid named Perk had disappeared. Death-filled cops had made him their boy. He had crapped all over himself. The lady he had dug the most had joined the lady he loved in selling him out to The Man. No, dammit, it sure didn't matter if a wino had gone out to get another drink.

In sudden anger he forced his arm up to the switch, snapping on the light. He pushed himself so that he rolled over the edge of the bed; then painfully he pushed his body upward. Shuffling like an old man, he made his way to the bathroom. There he undressed and examined his body in the mirror of the medicine cabinet.

No scars. Not even one bruise to tell the tale of his aching body. If anything, his body looked smoother. Only a very careful somebody who knew him well might tell that the smoothness was caused by swelling. They did good work, no evidence. Not one mark to show police brutality, except perhaps the swelling of his lips. But this he knew. It would take all the Browns and Sullivans in New York City to waste his black body. If they wanted to do him in, the next time, they had better use their guns.

Under the shower he thought of his threat to Ann Aimsley: "I'm coming back." Had he meant it? He had said it. And why not? She had brought him into a death trap. Two days and he had been caught, trapped by the haves. So he was caught. If anybody wanted to get him, that's where he'd be. Only the next time they wanted to mess with him they had better come shooting.

Then as the water beat full force on his back, his chest, his head, reviving him, he thought of Gail—she had come, too. She had come, too . . .

Back in his room, while Imamu was putting on his soiled clothes, he heard movements in the front bedroom. So, she was still at home. The thought of how he had wanted to hurt her, beat her that morning made him shrink inside himself. He had never wanted her hurt. He didn't now. Still, he wasn't about to be accused—not by anybody. Not again.

He put the light out to make sure it did not attract her attention and finished dressing. He heard her leave her room and move toward him. In a panic he scrambled to get out, scuttled to the front door, and fumbled in the darkness for the lock. As he rushed out, he heard her call. He slammed the door and rushed down the stairs. He walked quickly through the streets, not wanting to talk to anybody.

He was already on the train, on the way to Brooklyn, when he thought of Peter Aimsley. For a moment the thought of the man's strong arms and broad shoulders forced him to hesitate inside. For a moment he thought of getting off the train at the next station. But it was only for one moment. His cold, angry mood pushed away the thought, and he sat quietly, saying to himself: "If it comes to that, I'll just have to take the dude on, that's all. I'll just have to take him on."

Gail heard the car door slam. At the same time she heard her mother's whisper in the dark living room: "So he didn't come." Gail had been praying for Imamu to get there while her father was still out. Her mother's words gave her the first indication that she had been waiting for him, too.

Peter Aimsley had gone out with the detectives, Brown and Sullivan, while Gail was still asleep. They had gone to talk to neighbors and friends. She had wanted Imamu to come to at least thrash things out with her mother before her father's return. But now it was already midnight.

With dread Gail heard footsteps outside and, looking out of the window, saw Peter Aimsley and Mr. Elder walking toward the stoop. "I hope he doesn't come." Ann Aimsley kept her voice at a whisper. "I want to push my mistake—put him behind us."

"Imamu? Put him behind us? How can we do

that, Mother? Do you think you can just accuse someone and . . ."

"Gail, can't you see? It will only make it harder for us. . . ."

"For us?" Gail wanted to point out that it was her mother who had brought Imamu home. She had been the one to accuse him. If anyone had it hard, it was Imamu. But underlying Ann Aimsley's words was a plea for Gail's support. Her mother had a need to be justified that was so strong that quarreling might only stiffen her position against Imamu even more.

"Imamu is coming and he's going to help us find Perk." Gail spoke quietly, she hoped forcefully.

"What can he do that the police are not already doing?"

Gail wondered how to say that she had an image —a clear image—that Imamu would find Perk, and that there was nothing anyone could do to shake that belief.

She heard her father's key in the lock and she turned on the lamp on the table at her side. "Mother," she said hurriedly, "you know, bringing Imamu here was a great thing. All the girls, their parents, too, looked up to you because of it. How would it look if Imamu came back and was forced to go to Aunt Dora's to stay?"

Instinctively she knew she had found the right words. She had surprised a quirk in her mother's mind and now she was following it. But she could only hope . . . Her mother turned from her, away from the light. Gail looked past her mother and saw her father coming through the door, bringing with him the simplicity of his grief.

The lines of his square face had deepened, aging him. His eyes, those wondering, wandering little boy's eyes that were staring past her face, looked beaten, dulled. Those eyes asked questions: What have I done? In all my life, what have I done? Haven't I worked and worked? How did this happen to me?

His little boy's bewilderment caught at her heart. She wanted to answer those questions: Nothing, she wanted to say. You have done nothing but love us and make things good for us. We love you. She longed to go to him, touch him, rub his neck, his slumping shoulders, his back. But if she did, he would take her in his arms, crush her to him, hold her to his chest as though making up, through her, for his missing Perk. He had done so earlier when her mother had brought her home from the police station. And if he did it now she would cry. It would make it too hard to defend Imamu against him—when Imamu came.

She left the room. Bowing her head to escape her father's defeated eyes, she ran upstairs, carrying with her the weight of their despair. There, sitting on the edge of her bed in the darkness, she listened to the creak of boards bending under Mr. Elder's feet as he slowly mounted the stairs to his room. The silence coming from Perk's room across the hall beat loud against her ears. What had happened to all that talking? Wherever Perk was, was she still talking? Making someone laugh? Someone angry? Or was she silent . . . still . . . ? The image of a silent, still Perk, floating in the darkness around her head, made Gail double over in pain. The pain sharpened. Then, with a terrifying suddenness, she realized that she was hungry! Painfully hungry!

Nothing so ordinary as food ought to claim her attention. Not at a time like this! Jumping from the bed, Gail rushed to the window, stuck her head out and looked up and down the street, trying to keep her mind on Imamu's coming, on her sister, on the neighbors who had gathered at the front of the house earlier. But she was starving!

Her mother hadn't cooked. Routine in the house had been suspended. That was as it should be. No one ought to think of food at a time like this. But here she was, dying from lack of it. Gail stared hard at the big shadowy tree standing in front of the house. Was she really so selfish? People went for days without eating and survived, just as trees went without water for long periods of time and survived. She had to think beyond herself. Hadn't she always? But her stomach kept on griping.

What if she went down and fixed something? Would her parents eat? Or would they hate her for even thinking about food? God, did her feelings ever stay in harmony with her parents'? First she thought of Imamu, now of food.

With an effort Gail tried to bind herself to her parents' sorrow. But the darkness outside blurred into more darkness. She found herself running down the stairs, then stopping at the living room to call, "I'm going down to fix something to eat."

In the kitchen she opened the refrigerator and grabbed a slice of boiled ham. She crammed it into her mouth and chewed and swallowed, waiting for the relief it would bring.

"I'm sorry about dinner," her mother said, walking into the kitchen. "I'll get something . . ."

"No, let me," Gail said. It was too late to add the burden of cooking to all that had gone before. "A salad with ham all right with you?" Without waiting for an answer Gail took the ham, lettuce, tomatoes, and cucumbers out of the refrigerator.

Ann Aimsley's eyes followed Gail as she went over to the sink. Knowing her mother wanted to continue their talk, Gail turned the water on hard, letting it splash on the lettuce.

Her mother spoke over the noise. "You see, he didn't get here."

"What do you think that proves?" Gail asked.

"He said he would. You heard him . . ."

"And suppose he doesn't, Mother? Suppose he comes tomorrow, or the day after—then what?"

"He's not coming. He only said that to—"

"He said that to do what, Mother?" She cut off her mother to ask the question, forcing her to listen to her own words.

"Why are you against me, Gail? How do you know he's all he says that he is? How do you know that he didn't—"

"Didn't what?" Turning to face her, Gail saw the pain of her mother's thoughts sifting through her eyes. Nevertheless, she forced her question home. It was better to do it now, before Imamu came, before her father joined them. "Just what do you think Imamu did to Perk?" Gail's eyes were hard.

Ann Aimsley didn't answer; she couldn't. It was as Gail suspected: Her mother had not formed her vague ideas into anything concrete. She probably didn't want to. Finally, Ann Aimsley cried out, "I don't know! God, Gail, put yourself in my place. I brought that boy into this house . . ." She covered her face with her hands. Muffled sobs tore through her fingers. But instead of pity, Gail felt herself turn cold, withdrawing from her mother's pain. It seemed as though they had played this scene before.

"Why, Mother? Why did you bring him home?" Gail prodded her mother. "You didn't know him— you don't know him now."

"I was only trying to do good."

Yes. Those were the same words she had spoken about the artist, Lonnie. "Miss Ann Aimsley a big-timer now," Dora Belle used to say, teasing. "They call it patron of the arts." And her father used to laugh. "Ann ain't saying much, but I know it's costing me good money." It had: years of rent. And just like that, it was over: One of her father's suits had been missing. It was an expensive suit that her father never wore because it had gone out of style. When her mother had found out it was missing, she had accused Lonnie of selling it. Then she had asked him to leave.

Lonnie had been angry. He shoved at her the one thing he had of value—his painting. Her mother had taken it, perhaps thinking of selling it. "That's

what happens when you try to do good," she said
when he left the house.

Gail had been eleven. She had hated Lonnie's
leaving. He had been nice to her. She had known
him, it seemed, all her life. And she remembered
her mother's confusion when her father mentioned
to her later that he had given the old suit to a cus-
tomer. And she also remembered that Ann Aimsley
had never told her husband why Lonnie had left.

"But that was such a big step, Mother," Gail said.
What was her mother holding from them this time?

"I wanted to give the boy a chance. I ought to
have seen he was only a street boy——"

"Ann! You can't mean that!" Peter Aimsley stood
in the doorway, looking baffled. "That's mean business you talking. Hell, I'm from the street! You got
to have known something more—felt something
about that boy. Folks gives off them vibes. But you
don't just be going around accusing a stud, because
he's from the street . . ."

"Peter." She went to her husband, lifting her face,
begging him to share her confusion. "I—I try so
hard to be decent—but something always seems to
happen . . ."

God, didn't she remember Lonnie? Gail wondered. Had so many years gone by to make her
forget?

"He said he was coming back," Ann Aimsley
said. "And he didn't."

"What would that prove, if he did, Ann?"

"That he was innocent."

"How?"

"He's young. Sixteen. He wouldn't have the nerve . . ."

"But you don't know that. You don't know the minds of cats from the street."

"But, Daddy, you know. So you must know that Imamu had nothing to do with Perk's disappearing."

"I don't know nothing!" Peter Aimsley shouted. "I don't know nothing except my lil girl ain't here. You understand?" Suddenly tears rushed out of his eyes. He ignored them and kept shouting, "I don't want him around me! Just thinking that maybe he had something to do with Perk will make me kill him! Do you understand? I'll kill him with these!" He pushed out his work-hardened hands.

Gail gazed at the gnarled hands feeling their strength, the strength of the arms in which veins and muscles twisted themselves like vines beneath the skin, disappearing beneath the sleeves of the shirt to reappear as the strength of his neck, the support of his grim face. She looked into the reddened eyes . . . The doorbell rang.

Imamu followed Gail down the stairs to the kitchen and stood in the doorway looking at Ann Aimsley. She had turned to look at him, her back to the table, leaning on her arms for support. He knew they had been discussing him. The air around them smoldered; the heat rose between them and him. His heartbeat quickened, his breath spurted as though he had been running. Imamu reached for his pocket but then let his hand fall without a toothpick. He intended to play this scene without props—all the way.

He had come. They had done him. They were wrong as hell but he had come. The next move was on them. They could turn him out. Call the police. Tell him to go to hell. But one thing sure. He hadn't let a mother chase him or shit on his head. He was no chicken and he damn sure was no turkey. It was on them.

He hadn't thought out his attitude before. But it formed as he was standing there, keeping him cool while he stared at his accuser, waiting for her to move. This was the time for her to go for what she knew. Tell all. If she had something going on, why she had been good to him, why she had done him, let it all spill out.

Without looking he knew Peter Aimsley's fists were clenching and unclenching. He sensed the menace, but he kept looking into Ann Aimsley's intelligent eyes, teary now, in that gentle plain face, softened by that head of elegant gray hair. He stared hard into the face that he dug, the face he had gone all the way out for.

Time stretched between them, stretched and stretched, and when it could go no further, he heard her say almost under her breath, "Oh, you did come back. . . ." and realized that although she was looking at him she was sending out feelers to the others, waiting for their reactions. No one spoke, so she said louder. "Well, now that you're back—"

"Only until we find Perk." He cut her off. His

words seemed to say themselves. "Only until then."
He felt the danger ease, sensed the slump away
from anger of Peter Aimsley's shoulders.

And then he heard Gail say in a voice heavy with
relief, yet pretending to be light, "Anyway, you got
here just in time. I just fixed dinner."

15

"We'll go looking around, Imamu and I. Oh, Daddy, I know you've been around the last two days. But we—well, we can think of places that you can't. Well I mean . . ."

Gail kept talking. She had to go on, apologizing, coaxing, to keep a heavy silence from falling over the table. The rest kept trying, or pretending to try, to eat what had to be good food. Ann Aimsley had put herself out cooking: roast pork, greens, mashed potatoes, cornbread—the smells wafted up from the table. But apart from Gail, who ate too quickly to taste the food, the others were play-acting.

It only proved to Imamu that eating together just to keep a habit going didn't make it. He had escaped the habit for two days. The first night he had crashed into bed and his body—which ached even more the next morning—had challenged his will when he wanted to get out of bed. His body had won and he had slept another day. From the atmosphere that his coming had brought to the dinner table, it might have been better if he had just kept on sleeping.

Imamu kept his eyes on his plate as he ate. Once, feeling Ann Aimsley looking at him, he raised his eyes. Hers shied away. He looked at Peter Aimsley, who raised his eyes under his bushy, quivering eyebrows and tried to stare him down. But then he too looked away. The heaviness grew. Gail kept on talking. "I bet you think that we . . ."

Her father stood up so abruptly that his chair fell back. Throwing his napkin down on his plate, he walked out. The rest sat quietly, listening to his feet pounding up the stairs.

Gail stared bleakly at the food piled high in the serving dishes. Her words had run out. And as she had anticipated, the silence descended on them. Imamu got up, too. He pushed his chair back gently, walked slowly to the door, eased himself up the stairs—he didn't want to echo Peter Aimsley's frustrated stamping—and went out on the stoop.

It was a hot, humid June night. Imamu sat on the fourth step down and stared into the darkness. He felt suspended in time and space. He didn't belong, and he didn't want to think about wanting to belong. A gust of hot wind swung up the street, shaking the leaves of the trees so that they brushed against one another, creating an atmosphere, a hushed music that somehow went with his sense of not being. He leaned his head back against the top step, letting the air fan his sweating neck. The door opened and Gail came out to sit on the top of the stoop.

"God," she cried. "It's hard. I didn't realize how hard it was going to be." Imamu closed his eyes to block out the long legs, in the short white shorts swinging next to his head. For a few moments they were silent. Then Gail sighed and said, "It's so scary. To think that something—out there—can reach into our home and change it, change life as we know it, cause such pain. Imamu, I'm frightened. I walk home from school now, no longer sure. At dinner tonight I got the strangest feeling that something was going to happen—to us—to us all. Something even worse. Although what can be worse?"

Imamu stared hard at the darkness under his eyelids. He was trying to feel along with her. He couldn't. Everything had always been scary—to him, to the folks he knew. Everything worse was always happening. It was part of their lives, built in. The Iggys, the Browns, the Sullivans. Out there dudes and chicks, young and old, walking the streets had fear in their pores, heavy on their backs—a part of their lives to deal with, or give up living.

How to explain that? She'd never understand—never mind her year on him. Things he was born knowing, she'd never know. But that's the way her life was split.

"It's even worse for Daddy," Gail kept on. "He always felt that he could do anything—that he was in control . . ."

"He sure only thought it," Imamu said. "A cat can only go for what he knows—what he's got going for him . . ." He wanted to explain his words. But words were what he didn't have, never had.

"You can't blame him for thinking it," Gail said. "After all, Daddy's always accomplished what he set out to do."

"That ain't much," Imamu pointed out.

"Most people don't even accomplish that—"

"Now, I ain't saying he don't think it's much. Or that Mrs. Aimsley don't think it's something. I'm just saying he ain't never wanted but so much."

The heavy air closed down over Imamu's head along with her anger. He could read her thoughts: Who are you to say such things about *my* father? What have you got? What has your mother ever wanted? But she wasn't going to say it. She was thinking it, but she would fight against saying it.

He squinted up at the swinging leg, at the shorts that seemed to get whiter as the evening deepened, sharpening the contrast between the shorts and the brown legs. He liked that. But he closed his eyes to keep from enjoying it. That wasn't what he had come back for. That's not what he was about.

Yet he had to fight against the temptation to reach up and grab the swinging leg and bite it, so that they could end up wrestling until he pinned her to him, kissed her on the dark stoop. He laughed to himself. It was bad enough having to deal with Peter Aimsley's shifting eyes, his waiting anger. He wasn't about to deal with those fists.

Imamu sat up, looking up and down the tree-lined street at the neighbors who had brought out chairs. There weren't many. Most of the people on the block were secure in their air-conditioned houses, safe from the hot, humid air of the street. That made sense. Air conditioners kept the streets cool, too. The city ought to install air conditioners in all of the houses in Harlem and Bed-Stuy. Keep the streets safe and the population happy—in the summer time.

But that kind of thinking did not exist in the city or in the whole country. Seemed that folks set rules with evil intentions. Like fighting to keep young dudes from working and getting paid decent, then passing laws to keep old studs on the jobs. They liked to say old folks had more experience. But old folks don't go around beating in heads! Put young, poor cats to work, make them work. Force them to make money so they would have a reason to fight to keep the country and their money safe— for democracy.

Al Stacy liked to say: "Poor dudes tears up some streets. But get them college kids out of work and put them in the streets—they'd bomb neighborhoods—real gone neighborhoods, too.

"Uncle Sam knows what he's doing," Al Stacy said. "Keep the streets full of poor suckers—in their place. That keeps the jails running; troops at the reach of the army. Put poor dudes to work and screw the economy? All them policemens out a work? All them judges out a work? Them lawyers? And don't even start talking about them half-assed politicians. Baby, the life of the country depends on you being out of work!"

"What's wrong with a man trying to make his

family happy?" Imamu felt Gail's anger reaching out to him. He took a toothpick out of his pocket and put in his mouth, shaking his head. They actually sent kids to college to learn to ask simple questions. Happiness, what was all that about?

"So you happy?" he asked. "Then he ain't done so hot now, has he?"

"It's not his fault—"

"Ri-ight. He ain't had nothing to do with nothing."

He felt her anger mount. But he kept on. "And he ain't had nothing to do with Perk being where she is, or where she ain't. Or what she's feeling, or if she ain't. Happiness!" He bit hard on the wood in his mouth, knowing he had hit too hard. Why? He wasn't after Peter Aimsley.

Never mind that Peter Aimsley tried to pretend that the Invisible Man's name was Imamu. That was okay. He dug where the man was coming from. He had never pretended that he loved Imamu, the way the two women had—and then lined him to the cops. What he and Peter Aimsley had had together, they had snatched. Now the man guarded that with his silence. No, he wasn't hard on the dude at all.

"Look, Gail," he said in a gentler voice. "I guess what I'm telling you is that we—I might be from the street but I ain't dumb."

"I didn't say you were!"

Imamu shrugged. No, she didn't. Might not even

have thought it. Except she did. He changed the subject.

"Now we know that Perk ain't just missing," he said, getting back to the safety of their commitment. "And we know she ain't been hit by a car."

"And we know she wasn't kidnapped," Gail added.

"How do we know that?"

"Don't we?" Gail asked timidly, not wanting to upset him. "Who would kidnap her?"

"Never know what folks likely to do," Imamu answered.

"No one has asked for ransom."

"Maybe what they want from her ain't got nothing to do with money. See what I mean?"

"Rape?"

"Maybe."

"No!"

"But then maybe what they want with her, ain't got nothing to do with what we used to thinking's important. Might be something way out. Know what I mean?"

He waited for her to understand, knowing and hating that the words were confused in his mind and would come out unclear. "No, I don't," Gail answered quietly.

"Okay, let's go down like this." He stretched his mind to find parallels. "Now take those cops who pulled me in. Now, if Perk had been missing on Park Avenue, say, where them rich folks live—

those studs would have dug up the night trying to find her. They wouldn't be sleeping yet. On the other part of it—if, say, my old lady reported me missing in Harlem, them suckers would come, put a few words down on a dirty piece of paper, go to a bar, get a few, then go and hand that paper to the chief. Now that would have nothing to do with nothing but putting in some hours to get some pay —see what I mean?"

She thought a long time before saying, "I'm trying."

"Okay, let's do it this way," he said patiently. "Now, those cops who came to the house that night looked around, see. No big deal, right? They took me in. Probably they'd been fooling around the precinct, nothing to do, needed to do somebody real bad. Now that ain't had nothing to do with Perk, see? Oh, sure, they wanted to find her. But if they hadn't had that other thing going, they might have looked around a lil more. They wouldn't have settled for me—not with that little bit of evidence. See where I'm coming from?"

Imamu looked up at Gail, expecting to see a flash of understanding. He didn't. So he kept on. "They know guys like me, see? They meet us every day and pull us in. We both out there, dig. We are a part of their case. They know I ain't offing nobody, or kidnapping nobody. They know an Iggy from an Imamu. They know things just from being out there, get it? So they know I ain't into snatching or messing around with nobody. So they pulled me in for something else. Got that?" He waited. She waited.

"Now, I want out," he went on. "More than anything I want out. See? More than you want to see Perk, I want—" He put his hand up to ward off her protest. "Look, baby, I ain't done nothing. So I got to want out, Jack. But if I run—now I get it in the back, see? So I got to go along. See what I'm into?"

"No, I don't." Gail shook her head, not ready to believe.

"Look, those turkeys, they get paid to do a job, right? And more often than not they do a bad job. It takes more than they got going for them up there"—Imamu tapped his head—"they know it, and that gets them uptight. So they got to get their Joneses off. See? That's what they do when they put a hurting on me—and folks who ain't got nobody out there ready to squawk. They get their kicks.

"Which ain't got nothing to do with me—except that I'm available. It ain't got nothing to do with Perk. It ain't even got nothing to do with them, except for kicks, man, kicks. Now you see where I'm coming from?" he asked hopefully.

"But that's sick," Gail almost shouted.

"Ri-ight." Imamu settled back on his elbows, pleased he was finally understood.

Then Gail said, "I—I guess I'm just dumb, Imamu. I really don't understand."

Imamu started poking between his teeth with the toothpick. Damned if he was going through that one again. "Anyway," he said, "you know that Perk didn't just walk out into space. She went somewhere under her own steam with somebody—or to somebody."

"Why do you say that?"

"It's just got to be, that's all—especially around this place. Kids got habits, just like we dudes on the block got habits. Mornings we hit the streets knowing where to find each other. If one of us ain't around—let's say before one, afternoon—we know he's busted, dead, or got himself tight with a chick, dig?"

"Really?" Gail sniffed.

Imamu smiled. "Yeah. Same with Perk. She didn't do nothing far out of what she generally do. She moved just the same, or near the same as she's been doing—either by herself or with somebody that ain't no stranger. If not she'd have stuck out."

"What you are trying to say, Imamu, is that whatever Perk did, wherever she went, someone ought to have seen her?"

"Ri-ight. You got that."

But her long silence put him in doubt. Imamu shook his head. The girl said she was an English major. Then why did they communicate backwards? "Look, forget it," he said. "You ain't got to understand these things to be a fashion designer."

"What's that got to do with anything?"

"Means you ain't got the pressure to see things the same way us cats out there sees them."

"You are trying to say—"

"I ain't trying," he cut her off, getting angry in turn. "I said it!"

"But nobody saw her." Gail spoke in a little girl's voice.

"Wrong. Folks seen her. Folks who been seeing her seen her. And she did the same thing she usually do—at least on this street—or they would have looked."

"Do you hear yourself—?" She stopped when she heard Mr. Elder coming out on the stoop.

"Hey, Mr. Elder," Imamu called. "Howya doing?"

The tall man hesitated, his eyebrows under the black hat stretched out with an anxiousness to join them. But then he looked at Gail. Exposing his brown teeth in a smile, he touched his hat and went down the steps. Imamu kept looking at him as he walked up the block, his overcoat flapping in the breeze as he melted into the darkness.

"God, I hate that man!" Gail spoke as though she had been trying to contain herself.

"Why's that?"

"You can look at him and ask why?"

"He is a weird-looking dude," Imamu answered. "But that ain't no reason to hate nobody. I know lots of strange-looking studs out there. Big jokers. What he ever do to you?"

"I don't remember . . ."

"How's that?"

"I think when I was a little girl . . . I know I used to scream and run whenever he came around. But I can't remember . . ."

Imamu wanted to ask her if *she* heard herself. Instead he laughed. "That's crazy," he said. "All that time and you still talking about the cat's looks?"

"It has been long. He's one of my father's oldest friends. They were in the merchant marine together. He used to be a friend of Dora Belle's, too."

"Yeah?" Imamu smiled at the change-up of her words. "I figured something like that."

"That was before Jacques."

"Hey, what about Jacques?"

"What about him?" Gail replied slyly. "He is handsome. And I mean handsome."

"A young dude, too, I bet?"

"What do you mean, too?"

"Only that as good as she looks . . ."

"Jacques is certainly older than you."

He heard jealousy in her voice, and liking the sound, reached up to touch her swinging leg. The door opened and Imamu kept his hand up, pretending to inspect his fingernails.

"God, it's unbearable out here," Ann Aimsley said from the doorway. "Why don't you two come into the house?"

"Is there something you want me to do?" Gail asked.

"No, I did everything. I just thought you both might want to come in and keep cool. Your father is going out."

"Oh?"

"Yes, he's going to Dora Belle's."

Why did her loneliness remind him of his mother:

fearful, resentful, missing her child? At least Ann Aimsley had a husband, one who ought to understand. But then, the warm heaviness, the worn brown couch, the comfort of Dora Belle . . . Imamu closed his eyes. He kept them closed, even when the brisk smell of cologne told him that Peter Aimsley had come out on the stoop.

His foster father brushed past Imamu as he went down the steps. In the silence that lingered at the top of the stoop, Imamu sensed Ann Aimsley's wish to be going with her husband, trailing like vapor. "Why don't you take Imamu with you?" she called after her husband, substituting one wish for another.

Yes, she was an intelligent woman. She knew that she had to ease the strain, their straining to be natural, or the foundation of the house would crack.

But Imamu had not come back to go to Dora Belle's to eat from her bowl of fruits. He had come for only one thing. "Why don't you go with him, Imamu?" Gail urged softly. Trying, everybody trying. Imamu sat up and saw Peter Aimsley behind the wheel of the car, staring out into the dark.

He didn't want to say no to his wife. Nor did he want to deny Imamu. Whatever had been between them had been small, frail, indefinite. He trusted that part of himself that had felt it. He didn't want to be wrong. And, too, he didn't want to bring *their thing* into Dora Belle's living room.

"Go on, Imamu," Ann Aimsley said. Imamu stood up. And just when he thought it better to sit down again, Peter Aimsley looked at him. "Come on," he said. Imamu ran down the steps and got into the car.

Peter Aimsley tried Dora Belle's door and found it locked. "What the hell's going on here?" He rang the bell and they waited for the door to open. Then there was Dora Belle.

"Oh, God, Peter, you bring me boy to see me." After the quiet, the gloom, at the Aimsleys', Imamu had not expected the brilliance that was Dora Belle with her even-toothed, white smile, her bright red dress, the colors on the walls shouting along with her gay welcome. "But Imamu, how you ain't come before?" She reached out the door to drag him into the house. "But you ain't treat me nice a-tall. Ain't they tell you I want you to come—to stay? And you ain't even come to smile and say thanks all the same?" She hugged him to her.

Imamu sank into her softness, breathed in her perfume, felt the stirring in the pit of his stomach. He looked down into her black, teasing eyes, and his anger at her died. "But come in, huh." She pulled him into the living room, her face near enough to touch his, her eyes pinning him to her, her breath blowing on his chin, making invisible hairs crawl over his face all the way back to his neck. She dragged him down beside her on the couch.

"Tell me why you come?" she said, teasingly. "I know why Peter come." She looked at her friend, who had followed them and had slumped down in the chair at the other end of the coffee table. "Me rum ain't stand a chance once he know it here. But you—you miss me," she told him.

Self-consciously, Imamu shifted his eyes around the familiar room. He had been angry with her over the slip of the tongue to the cops. He had thought of being mean when he saw her, nasty. But he knew that talking had to be her problem. Things jumping out of her mouth—the same as Perk's—and then being sorry. In her house, looking at the colorful stuffed birds ready to take off out her window, he forgave her.

He remembered how he had run like a fool out of the house. What if he hadn't run? What if he wanted to stay now? Naw. He shook his head, put a toothpick in his mouth. He wasn't about anything but finding Perk.

But he had forgotten how good she looked. Seeing her in her shining red housecoat, her profile sharpened because her hair was pulled back and coiled, Grecian style, made him wonder why he had not thought to come there—to stay. Why not now? Whatever he could do from the Aimsleys' he sure could do from here, with no sweat.

The pulse beating in his stomach—that was hunger, real hunger. He had to be sick: He dug Gail, really dug her. Yet here he was with his stomach playing tricks at the feel of Dora Belle's soft flesh. He sat up straight. He was all about Perk.

But Dora Belle didn't mention Perk. She seemed determined to keep off the subject. "But look at he, Peter," she cried. "He pretty, yes?" Peter Aimsley looked at him and he blushed. "But look, nuh," Dora Belle cried in delight. "The boy miss me, for truth." Imamu felt embarrassment showing on his face. He wondered where to hide. Peter Aimsley saved him.

"Girl, go on and get me that rum I come after," he said.

"I getting it." She jumped up gaily as though determined to keep things happy. She went to the cabinet and came back with a bottle of rum and three glasses, which she set on the coffee table. "You letting him drink, Peter?" she asked.

What was with her—asking permission for him?

"Ask him yourself." Imamu threw Peter Aimsley a look of gratitude. He studied the slouching man in the chair. He looked more relaxed than he did at home. The tension tearing at him seemed to have eased, and despite the worry rumpling his face, he seemed a man who might stay forever young.

"Get some ice, nuh, Titi," Dora Belle cried impatiently. Imamu puzzled over that. But then someone who had been sitting in the wing-backed chair facing the window got up and shuffled over to stand at attention near the table. "Oh," Dora Belle said, "you ain't meet me new friend. He me new roomer —live in me house up the street."

Imamu's eyes locked with Peter Aimsley's. There was a moment of shocked pain in his eyes. They seemed to say, Now? At this time? You flaunt a new friend? Imamu felt shame, jealousy, then anger. Where did she get off squaring him out—right to his face?

"But what you want?" She jumped to the defensive. "What I should do? I ain't got nobody. I a woman alone." She leveled her eyes at the little, anxious-to-please, pointy-faced man and shouted, "But Titi, go get the ice, nuh." He shuffled out of the room and she turned her anger on Peter Aimsley. "But what you think? I waiting two, three years for one man? You must know, if I ain't got one thing to do with me time, I got a next. Look at me. You want that I dry up and get old waiting?"

Peter Aimsley stared at her. Imamu felt his blood pounding in his ears—then shrugged. He had decided to play it her way. "Seems that's what you life is about, Dora Belle, messing with men. Get them gone on you, then put them down. Ain't that what you done to my boy Elder?"

"Chu-ups." She sucked her back teeth contemptuously. "Ask for he? Don't talk about he."

"As hard as that cat went for you, gets sick and you . . ."

"I ain't tell he go get sick."

"But you got sick, too . . ."

"But I ain't get ugly," she said, waiting for him to say more.

But Peter Aimsley shook his head. "You learning a lesson first hand, man," he said to Imamu. "Better than I can teach you. It took me a lot longer to learn about women like Dora Belle."

"Don't listen to he." Dora Belle caught Imamu's chin and turned his face to her. "He think I corrupting you. But what wrong with that? A little good corruption is food for man." Imamu jerked his face away. The little man shuffled back into the room with a tray of ice and soda. Quietly, he placed it on the table and shuffled back to the wing-backed chair, sat down, and disappeared.

Peter Aimsley gave a short laugh. "I hope you know you're a damn fool, cutting Jacques loose." He poured rum over ice and handed her the bottle. "Merchant marines ain't always in control of their time. And with his folks all the way in Haiti—"

"I ain't care if he dead."

"Too bad. That engagement locket sure did look regal sitting up there on them magnificent boobies."

Dora Belle's glass brimmed over. She set the bottle down with a bang. "Don't trouble me head over that blasted man," she shouted. "I got trouble enough with me houses. But Titi," she called. "Go bring me a rag to wipe this table, nuh." Once again the little man dug himself out of the chair.

"And what's with the house?" Peter Aimsley asked. "Those men coming back?"

"No, but I get me some next ones. It hard, I tell you. You'd think I pay people with thanks instead of good money."

Peter Aimsley put his half-empty glass down and stood up. "Well, you know I'm around if you need—"

"But you ain't going already?" Dora Belle cried. Her anger died down.

"Yeah, I got to get back to the house." He moved restlessly around the room. And Imamu felt it there, alive—what she had wanted to keep down rising as though through the floorboards. "And what you going to do there? And Ann . . . ? Why ain't Ann come . . . ?"

"Ann? Ann is home waiting—waiting and praying."

"Praying . . . ?" Dora Belle's face twitched. "Praying . . . oh, God! But I hurting, too. Why it happen? Why it happen to she? Perk, me little darling. I did love that child. She was me heart. Me heart." She covered her face with her hands and rocked back and forth, moaning.

Peter Aimsley's eyes reddened, and when Imamu tried to look into them again, they shifted away. "Talk to you tomorrow," he said to Dora Belle and walked out. Imamu followed. They left as they had come: strangers.

16

Imamu stared at the painting of the stormy sea. He was impatient, ready to move, to go, to get out and run like wild through the streets. Going to sleep, getting up, going to sleep, getting up, and the time, like sand, was shifting over the minds of people, covering traces of everything that might lead to Perk. He had passed days around her school, watching kids, studs who hung around, trying to get vibes. Nothing!

In a way he blamed it on Dora Belle. He couldn't get her out of his mind—or little Titi, in that wing-backed chair. She had done him. Really done him. Angrily he stared at the picture, hating her, hating himself for being a square, moved by her games.

And then suddenly he wasn't angry. Only curious. Because he found that he was looking at bodies. Hundreds, maybe thousands of bodies, twisted there in the dark beneath the raging surf. Bodies made up the swirl of darkness. He stood transfixed. Every day he had been looking at the painting, and this was the first time he had really noticed.

Walking to the center of the room, Imamu looked at the painting. From there it seemed only a picture of a storm at sea. Slowly he moved forward, noticed the matchstick legs, saw when they jumped into meaning. He got closer still and saw the heads. And then closer to the bodies curled into one another, creating the denseness, as though beaten into one mass by the force of the pounding surf. He was dizzy.

Every time he looked at the painting he saw something new. The dude had taken six years to paint it. He had to be crazy. He wanted everyone who looked at it to jump out of their freaked-up minds!

"Where are you and Gail going?" Ann Aimsley's voice made him jump. He backed toward her, his eyes still on the painting.

"To talk to neighbors."

"What do you really think you can learn from them?"

"Trying," he answered.

"You seem to like that painting," she said.

"Yeah, ain't it something?"

"It took enough time . . ." Somehow he knew that she hadn't seen what he had in the picture. He wanted to explain to her what he had seen. But Gail came into the room.

"You ready, Imamu?" Gail asked.

"Yeah, come on, let's get out of here. Let's go." He was filled again with a sudden urgency, the need to get started, to finish what they had to do. He rushed her out of the house.

Outside, he grabbed her arm. "I got to be right about this," he said. Then feeling the thinness of her arm, he squeezed, moved his hand playfully up and down, testing her muscles. Gail snatched her arm away. Imamu grinned as she headed down the street.

"Like I was saying"—he fell into step next to her— "folks seen Perk that day. They had to because she did leave the house. The reason they don't remember is because nothing happened."

"Everybody knows that Perk is missing, Imamu," Gail said. "That would have made them remember. If not when the police asked, then soon after. They would have come to tell us."

"Okay." Imamu let her have that point. "But you got to agree that she left the house. Right?"

"Why go over that again?"

"And we got to agree that no car hit anybody on this block that morning, there were no earthquakes, no floods, no fires, no strangers hanging—"

"Why no strangers?"

"Because these folks around here would not have missed a stranger," Imamu said, thinking of his first day when he stood under the tree.

"No," Gail admitted. "They don't miss much."

"So whatever she did, she did on her own. In

other words, she did almost what she did most days."

"Almost?"

"Yeah, almost. But that almost was something that seemed natural enough not to stick on anybody's mind. Or at least not everybody's mind."

"Everybody?"

"That's right. Because somebody on this street saw her."

"Why do you say that?"

"Like I say—that almost. Look, Gail, she had to have done that almost. She ain't here."

Together they went up the steps of a brownstone a few houses down from theirs. "Mrs. Dixon was one of the first West Indian families to move on the block," Gail said. "She's raised a family of five and has grown grandchildren and a few great-grands."

Imamu rang the bell. "By now everyone must have forgotten what they saw," Gail said.

"Not true." Imamu shook his head. "By now, they'd be making up things to remember."

The door opened. "Good evening, Mrs. Dixon," Gail said to the small, brown and gray woman at the door. "I wonder if you'd mind us asking a few questions—Imamu and I."

"Gail, what a surprise." The woman stepped back to let them enter. "You want to ask about Perk. I have nothing but time. But I don't have anything to tell. Let me fix some tea for you," she said.

"No, thank you, Mrs. Dixon. I—we—you did meet my foster brother?"

"No, but I have seen him. Many times going and coming." She smiled at Imamu as she led them into her overfurnished living room.

The furniture, like Mrs. Dixon, was from another time. It was big, heavy, decorated with starched doilies and homemade cushions. Boxes were packed and crowded into all the available space. The photographs on the walls were so faded, they seemed to be begging to disappear into the past, but like the boxes and the furniture, they held on for her sake.

"Have some candy," she offered, opening one of the boxes on the overcrowded coffee table. They both shook their heads.

"Imamu thinks that maybe on the day that Perk disappeared, maybe, just maybe, one of the neighbors might have seen her doing something that might prove important—"

Mrs. Dixon, sat straight, like a schoolgirl ready to be tested. "I don't know . . ."

"It's been a while now, I know," Gail prompted. "It was the Memorial Day weekend. That Friday there was going to be a party at Perk's school . . . she had dressed up . . ."

"But Perk was always so dressed up. Ann sent both of you girls to school looking so nice—that is until you started with those—pants."

"But this day was special," Gail said. "Perky had on a new dress . . ."

Mrs. Dixon thought for a moment, but only for their sake. "I don't remember, Gail. Actually, I tried to think—the policemen were here, you know. I told them all I know."

"What was that?" Imamu leaned forward.

"I told them I hadn't seen Perk that morning. And that I saw you"—she nodded to Imamu—"going out with your hand tied up. But that was later. I was on the stoop and saw you going down the block. You had a brown paper bag." She said it like an indictment, then looked closely to see Imamu's reaction. "But I didn't see Perk. You know these television shows, they have these talk shows. . . . But not so long ago I used to be at that window, or on the stoop, looking at the children going off to school. Perk with little Babs or else with Mr. Elder . . ."

"Mr. Elder!" Gail exclaimed. "Perk and Mr. Elder? Are you sure?" Her face glowed with anger.

"Of course. All the time," Mrs. Dixon said, surprised. "When she walked with him, she never thought to look at me or wave, she'd be so busy talking. And that child can talk. Never let the poor man get a word in. But then, he was so fond of her. Why not? He's known her all her life."

Fear widened Gail's eyes so Imamu rushed to say, "But you don't remember them on that day, right?"

"Well, it's like I said. I didn't go out until much later. Then I saw you . . ."

Gail waited until they were outside before she exploded. "Mr. Elder, of course. It makes sense.

If things hadn't taken that stupid turn with the policemen taking you in, I would have thought of it."

"What makes sense, Gail?" Imamu tried to calm her. "That lady ain't seen them together that day. She ain't even looked out her window—not until I hit the scene."

"It has nothing to do with what she said. It's a feeling."

"And you feel ... ?"

"That he has something to do with Perk's disappearance. I have always felt there was evil in the man. Can't you see, Imamu? Him talking to her—outside."

"He lived in your house," Imamu said. "Why shouldn't he be friendly?"

"He never acted friendly *in* the house."

"Not in front of you, maybe. Not the way you acted toward him."

"Can you look at that man and treat him any other way?" Gail's voice faltered. "Imamu—I have always known that he might do something . . ."

"Look, I know the dude acts weird," Imamu said, annoyed. "But that ain't reason to think he's into anything. Hell, that's what the cops did to me. They looked at me and hauled me off. They didn't like my looks. Now ain't that a mess?"

"That was different."

"How?"

"You were innocent!" Even as she said it she must have realized how she sounded. But she kept on. "I knew you were innocent."

"You talking about feelings." Imamu laughed. "So happens you were right about me, but you don't always have to be right."

"About you?" she asked. "I'll always be right about you, Imamu. . . . I don't want you to ever leave . . ."

Imamu looked down at her round face with its big brown eyes, her mouth, determined, yet so girlish. He wanted to hug her to him, mess with her hair, chase her down the block, kiss her, thank her for being in his corner. Instead he said, "About Mr. Elder. Look, Gail, we said we were going through this block. What say we do that first, before we get into feelings? Okay? That way we can get a whole picture and take our pick. Now, I ain't saying you wrong. Just let's try it my way."

He knew it was hard on her to let him take the lead; she was so used to being the intelligent one. She shrugged. "Let's go talk to Mr. Miller." They crossed the street and walked over to Mr. Miller, who was sitting on his stoop. He saw them coming and called as they walked up, "Hey, you kids, see you all go over to Mrs. Dixon. What you doing? Raising money?"

That block said things to Imamu. He didn't know exactly what. There it was in the middle of Brooklyn, USA, with its trees planted so close, its brownstone houses so closed in, that its one other American family had his Southern accent flavored West Indian.

"No, Mr. Miller," Gail said. "We're trying to find out who saw my sister the day she disappeared."

"That's the morning after he come." Mr. Miller raised a hand toward Imamu, but let it fall back on his large stomach.

"Yeah," Imamu answered.

"That's right." The big man reared back on the stoop, giving his stomach space to settle between his widespread legs. "You'd think the police would have asked me. Hell, I was right out there when they come that next day, ain't even look my way. And, you know, I sees everything going on around here. But they ain't asked me nothing. Now you know, from here, I can see clear down to Mrs. Briggs's, on this side—and damn near to the corner on that, especially in winter when them leaves ain't around. Yeah, spring, summer, gets hard. All the same, I know what's happening. But them police, I ain't told them nothing, neither."

"Then you did see her?" Gail asked, getting excited.

"Who?"

"Perk."

"Well now . . ." Mr. Miller scratched his head.

"Man"—Imamu spoke impatiently—"what was you gonna tell them bulls when they asked?"

"Well, I reckon I did see her. See her all the time. Now the day he come"—he nodded to Imamu —"I was finished messing with them garbage cans. Almost missed him. Took a couple out back and when I come, he's going up the steps. That day now—seen Miss Perk . . . went to school in the car . . . you, too," he said to Gail. "Your father took you all."

"What about the next day?" Imamu asked.

"Well, this the way things generally happen." Mr. Miller put his arms around his stomach. "Aimsley, he come out about seven, seven-thirty. Gets in his car and drive off. Next to go, you." He nodded to Gail. "Always in a hurry, always late. Then the lil one—or sometimes it's Elder. If the lil one come first and Elder ain't around, more than likely she go after her friend Babs. If Elder come out first and she see him, she run after him. That's the way it happen."

They'd talk all day and he'd never admit to not having seen Perk, to not knowing. "Then Mr. Elder don't come out every day?" Imamu asked.

"No, days he don't leave the house—not even to go play his numbers. He play down the way with Gus. But he's a sick man. Now, that day I ain't seen him leave but I seen him when he come back."

"Come back?" Gail said to pin him down.

"Why, sure," the big man answered. "He goes up that way, do what he got to, play his numbers, and comes right back up the block before the morning's over."

As they walked away, Imamu put his hands in his pockets; he was thinking. But the excitement in Gail kept pulling at him. He didn't want her to talk, didn't want to hear what she had to say, but she said it anyway. "Doesn't it sound strange that on the morning he didn't see Perk, he didn't see Mr. Elder go out either?"

"We weren't supposed to talk about it, remember?"

"I don't care. The more I hear, the more I know that Mr. Elder has something to do with it. Listen—" She ran to stand in front of him to force him to listen.

"Look." Imamu tried to discourage her. "Just because he walked Perk—"

"You have to know him as well as I do to understand—"

"Understand what? Girl, we don't know no more now than when we started." Anxiety had brightened her eyes. She was shaking. He took her hand and pulled it through his arm.

"We know that Mr. Elder walks with Perk—"

"Then does what he's got to do, plays his numbers, and comes back home. Okay? So you are finding out things that you ought to have been knowing."

"But I do."

"You as much as admitted to not knowing. Man's been living in your house for years. You don't like him, don't trust him, closed your mind against him so tight that you didn't even know he walked the streets. Scared. You scared like one of them birds what stick their heads in sand—what you call them?"

"Ostrich."

"Ri-ight. Maybe if you got to know the dude, you might like him."

"Never!"

"Oh, come on. You can't even remember nothing he done."

"But I do! I do remember, Imamu." She stepped in front of him and stared into his eyes. "Imamu, Mr. Elder tried to kiss me when I was a little girl. I fought and fought. But he actually tried to kiss me!"

17

Taking Gail's hand, Imamu pulled her along, letting what he had just heard work through his mind. "How old were you?" he finally asked.

"I can't remember."

"Are you for real? Were you old as Perk? Older? Younger?"

"I guess I might have been younger."

Halfway up the block Imamu stopped. "Look, we're going the wrong way." Changing directions, he pulled her back down the block.

"What are you thinking?" she asked.

"Way I see it," he said, "Perk came down this way. Somebody down this way had to have seen her."

"What has that got to do with Mr.—"

"With what you just told me? Nothing." He felt the pull of her hand to get away and tightened his hold. He knew she was upset and angry, but he couldn't let her change his plan. His brain was full of little worlds, circles bumping into one another, sending him in directions he had to take.

They walked by Mr. Miller again, and the fat man called out, "Oh, went the wrong way, huh?" Imamu waved and kept going. Gave him something to tell for the next twenty years. It was sure he did see everything—almost.

"Are you sure you want me with you?" Gail's small voice showed her peevishness. "I guess you call this a part of your street thing." She hit out when he didn't answer.

"Ri-ight." He tightened his hand on hers again. "See"—he slackened his pace to explain—"long as we guys were in our usual place, where we hung, no one looked, broke their necks so they couldn't see us. But the second we guys drifted—took one step out of our place—hell, folks got cross-eyed from looking, got chicken skin, hairs got to raising over their heads. They marked us good in their thinking. Now, we been looking more up the block because we figured that Perk more than likely went that way."

"But you're the one who said that she did what she usually did."

"Ri-ight. That the house Babs live in?" He pointed to a brownstone.

"Yes," Gail answered. When he walked right by it, she asked, "Why aren't we going in?"

"We know everything they know, right?"

He felt her sulking and stopped to look down at her hurt, dark, pretty face. Pulling her to him for what he intended to be a consoling hug, his body felt suddenly big, broad, at the feel of her slimness against him. He held her tight, making her respond to his heart slapping against his chest. He wanted to tell her how great she was to let him do the thinking when she was nothing but a bunch of brains. He only hugged her tighter.

"It's something you said." He played up her part, to ease her doubts, then realized that it *had been* something she had said. "To Mrs. Dixon. You said that Perk had on a *new* dress. Mrs. Dixon said that you all always look good. But Perk's dress was new, Gail. These folks on this street, lonely old folks, ain't got nothing to do but look. If Perk had a dress on one time these folks would see it, see how it was buttoned, where the pleats were, all that. That's all they got to do, look at television and neighbors. Might even call your old lady: 'Ann,' they'd say, 'I see you got Perk another new dress. You sure spoil her,'—something like that. Dig where I'm coming from? How many times you hear that?"

"Lots," Gail admitted. "But if you'd listen, Imamu . . ."

"I'm listening. Ain't I listening?" And when she didn't answer, "It's just that we got to see this plan out, right? And this street, it's got two ends, right?"

"Right."

He squeezed her hand, kept squeezing her hand and then she squeezed back. Everything was all right. They walked down the block holding hands. He had never held hands before. He liked her. He really liked her.

They walked to the corner, then started walking

back. They stopped at the first house, a red brick house surrounded by hedges that turned the corner. "Good evening, Mrs. Briggs." Gail greeted the woman working in the garden at the side of the stoop. The woman peered from under her wide-brimmed straw hat.

"But who is it?" she asked, not able to see in the soft evening light.

"Gail. Gail Aimsley."

"Oh, my dear," Mrs. Briggs stood up and opened the gate for them. She stood looking up at the tall girl, a smile spreading her tiny wrinkles smooth. "What a big girl."

"Do you know my brother?" Gail asked.

"Brother!" Mrs. Briggs looked at Imamu, puzzled.

"My new brother," Gail explained. "He's only been with us a short time."

"Oho, yes, to be sure. Quite a few families make a little here and a little there"—her voice dropped to a whisper—"even on this very block, never mind what they say." She smiled vaguely at Imamu. "But the Aimsleys are nice, yes?"

Embarrassed, Imamu looked from her to the large garden where she had been working. "Nice flowers," he said. She gazed around.

"Yes," she said, after a few seconds. "It's me joy—since Mr. Briggs gone. Is so I does spend me life."

"I'm sorry," Gail said. "I heard . . ."

"What to do?" The little old woman sat on the stone stoop, her head bowed, her cotton dress spread out around her. Imamu and Gail stood waiting, uncomfortable, for her moment of grief to pass. But when she raised her head, her eyes were flashing, the wrinkles burned out of her face by anger.

"Oh, God, but that was a wicked man, you hear?" she cried. "He bring me here from me good home in Jamaica. He sit me down in this house and from the day I did come, he gone. Gallivanting. Every day! And every night I did say to he, 'But Mr. Briggs, how you does take me from me country and bring me to this man's land just to go out and leave me every night, every night so. Is dead you want me to dead, Mr. Briggs?'

"And he laugh and say, 'But Lilly, you living good, yes? And ain't I buy you this house and this garden? What you want from me life? Ain't I work hard to treat you like a queen?' And the man gone. Leaving me here lone, lone, lone."

She sighed, looking up the street wistfully, thinking back to those dreams, dreams that had been cracked on the bricks of the beautiful old house.

"Year in, year out, it did happen so, until I make up me mind, good! Then I dry me mouth and close me mouth and I ain't wet it again with one word to he. You see, I make up me mind to dead, dead, dead. I had to show he, you see, that he cannot take a woman away from she good home with she father and she mother to bring she in this man's town and set she down to leave she alone, lone, lone.

" 'Lilly,' he say to me, 'how come you ain't talk to me? Ain't I bring you to this country? And ain't I work hard, hard, hard to buy this house so you can live good? And that garden that you does work in, ain't it the loveliest garden you did ever see? And ain't I treat you like a queen? So how come you ain't want to talk to me?'

"Me? I ain't talking to he a-tall. I waiting for he. I want he to see me stretch out on me bed, dead, dead, dead. Because you see, I ain't leave me mother house and me father house to come to this place to sit in no house alone, lone, lone."

They sat, Imamu and Gail, on the stone steps of the old brick house—the biggest and probably, at one time, the grandest house on the block—listening to her soft, frail voice. As they listened, the dusk approached, falling around them, holding them to the stoop, forcing them to hear the tangle of simplicity, so foreign to him yet so familiar, imprisoning them in a sort of suspense, waiting for what they both knew had to be a most illogical ending.

"Forty years, I did keep he house," the sweet-faced woman said, smiling. "Forty years I did cook he food and wash he clothes and keep he house clean. And is true I did play he wife in bed when he want. But not one word did cross these lips." She crossed her index fingers and kissed them. "Not one word so long as he see fit to leave me and go out gallivanting in the night. For I ain't leave me father house and me mother house to come to this cold country to stay by meself alone, lone, lone. And I ain't care how much he does say, 'But Lilly, ain't I bring you to this great land, and ain't I buy house with garden, and ain't I treat you like a queen? So how come I ain't hear the sound a your voice all these many years?'

"And I sew. I make me long white dress to stretch out in. And I sew the sheet to spread me bed, and I practice what way I want me hand to cross when he does come to find me dead.

"And it *he* get sick! All that rum, you know. He get the diabetes, and he liver gone, and he kidney ain't work good again. So he stay home. And I take good care of he. I bathe he. And I feed he. Rub he back with bay rum. And I make he sheet smell sweet, sweet. And I make he clothes all soft and good to he skin. Oh, I treat that man like a king. I talk to he: 'I glad you home now, Mr. Briggs. I so glad you home. Because you see, I ain't leave me mother house and me father house to come here in this place and sit all by meself alone.' And he say to me: 'Lilly, I bring you here to this big, rich man country. I buy the biggest house on the street. You got the biggest garden. Ain't I treat you like a queen? Ain't I make you happy, Lilly? Ain't I make you glad?' I was so pleased to say to him: 'Now, Mr. Briggs, the happiness coming now.'

"And just so, the other night, from me sleep I hear this thing in he throat. I jump up. I put on the light. And he breathing so . . ." She made loud gasps in her throat. "I grab he shoulder and shake he so. 'No, Mr. Briggs,' I say. 'Don't go. Don't you go leave me.' And just so he pass. I shake he and shake he. 'Mr. Briggs, Mr. Briggs,' I call he back," she cried angrily. " 'But how you does go and leave me? How you does do this thing to me? How you take me from me mother land and me father land and bring me to this damn country and set me down in this cold, concrete street and then kindly take your leave, leaving me alone, lone lone? Oh, God, but how you does do this thing to me?' He ain't answer. He ain't answer. He ain't answer . . ."

The tale ended, but they sat on. At last, reluctantly, they rose to their feet, conscience-stricken for having to go, for having to leave her alone. And then Gail said: "Mrs. Briggs, we . . . Imamu and I sort of thought that maybe you might help us with something that might lead to the reason for my sister's disappearance."

"Your sister?"

"Perk."

"Disappeared? I ain't hear nothing about that. Why just the other day I see Perk."

"You saw her!" Imamu and Gail said together.

"Ye-es, walking down that side of the street. I remember well. My azalea was still in bloom and I say to meself, 'There goes that sweet little Perk, she stand out from me hedges good in that yellow dress.' It ain't often all you does come down this way, you know. So I say to meself: 'I bet she coming to pay she respect to that rascal now that he done gone for good.' But she ain't look me way. She hurry down the street like she ain't got one thing in she head . . ."

18

A question here, a question there, and the orderliness of Gail's mind was crumbling. She had walked out of the house one person and was going back another. First, remembering her struggle against Mr. Elder. Then her weakness when Imamu hugged her surprised her, even frightened her. And then there was Mrs. Briggs and her strange tale.

For Gail, and probably for everyone on that street, Mr. and Mrs. Briggs had been the perfect couple. White-haired Mr. Briggs was handsome, loud talking, loud laughing, a gentleman from another time, another place, begging his page in history. Living in their big corner house, they were the epitome of success. God, what a betrayal!

The gentle street, its orderly row of houses, its shadows pulsed with secrets as threatening as her memory of Mr. Elder, as deceptive as the Briggs' perfect life. Nothing on the street was what it seemed.

Glancing at Imamu, Gail wanted to talk to him about how she felt, hear what he had to say. But Imamu's face, too, held nothing but secrets. Suddenly she wanted to get home, have the walls she knew close around her, talk to her mother, share their grief about missing Perk.

As they neared the Aimsley house, Gail ventured to ask, timidly, "We do know more now than we did before?"

"Ummm." Imamu grunted.

"Why was Perk going that way?"

"Huh?" Then he heard. "Dora Belle lives down that way."

"But she wouldn't be going to Dora Belle on a school morning."

"The subway is down that way."

"Why should Perk be going to the subway?"

"Don't know. It may be she just decided to go the long way around to get to school." Imamu was obviously distracted, too deep in thought to communicate.

"That's silly. Why don't you want to admit that that is the way Mr. Elder comes?"

"You mean that she walked down to meet him?"

"No." He had a way of making her suggestions sound silly.

"Could be she had something she wanted to do—something she wanted to keep secret."

"Perk and I never had secrets," Gail said.

"You didn't!"

Why should he be surprised? They were sisters. "No, we didn't."

"You mean you told her everything you and your friends did?"

"Not everything. She's a little girl."

"Ri-ight."

Gail looked up, trying to see through the shadows. "She never told me about Mr. Elder . . ." She hesitated.

"You mean that they walked together?" Imamu asked. "I don't see her thinking that a secret. She had to come out to go to school. Elder had to come out to do his thing—what's the big deal if they walked together?"

Hadn't he understood the importance of what she had told him about Mr. Elder? Maybe he hadn't really heard. Maybe he didn't care. She thought of herself in his arms, of the strange sensation in her thighs, her pounding heart. God, over this young boy?

"You wouldn't understand," she said after a short silence. "Women have a deeper sense of these things —intuition, you know?"

Imamu kept twisting the toothpick around his teeth while they walked up the steps to the door. "You do admit such things exist?" she asked as he pushed it open.

"Like what?"

"If I agree with your street thing—don't get me wrong, I do—then you must agree that there is a thing called intuition."

Imamu stared at her, then nodded. "Gotcha, gotcha. Ri-ight. Ri-ight." Which did not answer her question, but before she could press him, he disappeared into the living room. For a moment she wanted to follow him, but familiar sounds in the kitchen drew her down the stairs.

Ann Aimsley had just cleaned the refrigerator and was putting food back into it. Gail stood letting the familiar ease into her, tying her emotions together. It was good to be home.

"What time is it?" her mother asked, pushing the meat tray into the box and closing the door. A tightness in her throat kept Gail silent. So much had happened, was happening to them, yet there she was falling back into routine, ready to support the family misery. What word was there for her mother but brave? Sure, she made mistakes—who didn't? Gail moved over to her, wanting to show tenderness, appreciation.

"I had no idea it was so late." Ann Aimsley glanced at the wall clock. "I haven't even bought meat. I must run to the store. What do you want for dinner?"

"Hot dogs and beans?" Gail said, wanting to make it easy.

"What!" Ann Aimsley cried. "And have your father hand me my head? Heavens, don't I have enough of a time keeping this home together?" Then, realizing her reaction sounded hysterical, she added, "Not that I think . . . I mean . . . Dora Belle is such a fantastic woman. Nothing gets her down. She's so young . . . so vital. Beautiful . . ."

"Mother! You're jealous!" Gail cried out.

"What a thing to say." Her mother tried to laugh. She turned away, pulled off her apron, and took a long time to hang it in the closet. When she turned back she was smiling. "Look, if you want franks and beans, that's what you get. I'll get steak for Peter. Go and ask Imamu what he wants."

Stunned, Gail walked up the stairs and into the living room. Imamu had gone. Going to the door, she opened it in time to see him running down the steps. "Imamu," she called, "what do you want for dinner?"

"Food," he called back and kept on going, heading down the block. Stepping back into the house, Gail bumped into her mother.

"What does he want?" Ann Aimsley asked.

"Franks and beans."

Her mother evaded her eyes but Gail, realizing that her mother had been crying, blocked her way out of the door. She searched her face, seeing, as though for the first time, the tightness, the ropelike veins on her thin neck, the tired lines around her eyes. Tears rose to her mother's eyes. "Oh, my God, when will this all end, Gail? How?" Then, pulling herself tall, she tried a laugh, wiped her eyes, and went out, looking the same as she always looked.

Mother—jealous of Aunt Dora! This was crazier than Mrs. Briggs' tale. Her mother and father were the other perfect couple. Nothing was ever supposed to happen to that pair. And her godmother . . . ? They had been friends forever!

Gail started to go back to the kitchen but suddenly the thought of the spotless germ-free atmosphere there repelled her. She went instead into the living room, and refusing to sit on the plastic covers, paced up and down. She went to the window and stood looking out into the darkening day, listening to the familiar voices of people as they walked by.

How long had it been going on? Since Perk? He had been going to Dora Belle nights since Perk. Or had it been going on forever? She heard again the plaint of Mrs. Briggs' voice. Gail stared around the spotless room, so cold in its cleanliness, its order. She looked around at the reproductions of the great paintings on the walls. Then she looked at the one original. It reminded her of—of Imamu.

He belonged here with the painting! With the spotless house, the tireless quest for perfection. Perfection gone astray—a distortion—like Lonnie. Like Mr. Elder.

Her sudden insight frightened her. Yet she moved toward the door and stood there, holding on to the door frame, trying to halt her moving feet. But suddenly, knowing one thing, she had to discover more. Her body pushed her on. She stood at the stairwell, staring up to the upper floors, listening over the pounding in her ears. She heard only silence, which expanded as she climbed the stairs. Like an automaton she climbed, trying unsuccessfully to assemble the fragments in her brain. And her body, light, weightless, kept moving up. At every step her instinct instructed her to turn, to run back down, fly down, jump down. But her body kept moving up—past her bedroom, up past the range of the air-conditioning, up into the ovenlike heat of the top floor.

Sweat jumped out over her; her blouse stuck to her back. Her underarms itched. Her breath came in short spurts as though she had been running. Up she went, to the top step, then to his door. Her mind cleared a little. What did she expect to find? A clue? What clue?

If only Imamu had stayed. If only she had waited for him. Whatever he thought, no matter how he disagreed, he'd never have let her do this foolish thing—not alone. Her mother? She'd never understand. Her father? He'd be furious! She backed away from the door, toward the stairs. Then she remembered, as if it had happened the day before: the feel of his body, his hands reaching for her, his prickly unshaven face pressing against hers, his mouthwash breath blowing into her face as she struggled. And for the first time she allowed herself to see Perk lying somewhere—raped.

But why did she have to be alone! It seemed it had always been her struggle against him. Her word against his. In this her mother and father had always been united against her. *Had Perk had to struggle alone, too?*

Terrified, she went back to his door. No sounds. She knocked. No answer. She pushed open the door, wide. For a moment she stood at the threshold looking around, and then she stepped in, hurriedly closing the door behind her.

The tidiness of the room struck her after she switched on the light. The single bed was covered by a tightly drawn cotton spread; in spite of the heat, woolen blankets were folded neatly at the foot. The dresser was bare except for a comb and a brush. Two straight-backed chairs flanked the window. The floor was polished to a gleam. Somehow, Gail had pictured a room as disorderly as her own, a room where something might have fallen and been forgotten, waiting to be discovered by a resolute seeker. Now, having to search through closed drawers and closets, she felt like a criminal.

Then she noticed the pictures. Female nudes in different poses had been cut from magazines, framed, and hung on all the walls, even over the bed. Gail's lips went dry, her hands grew clammy. She stilled the urge to run, and moving quickly to the closet, opened the door and stood looking in. Only two suits hung there. One hat, on the shelf, one pair of shoes, and a pair of slippers, on the floor. No room for concealment.

Moving next to the dresser, she opened the two top drawers. She found a half-dozen handkerchiefs, well ironed, shoelaces, buttons, needles, and thread. The long drawer beneath held four starched shirts, laid side by side in laundry-room exactness. How strange for a man to be living here for so many years and to have so few possessions. Even the magazines from which he had cut the nudes were nowhere in sight.

In the center drawer, Gail found socks, two belts, and some ties, folded and lying neatly on top of each other. Gail knelt, thinking. Something hovered at the edge of her mind. She was looking at something and not quite seeing it. Then it came to her that she was looking at an uninhabited room. The clothes in the drawers and the closet seemed no more than props. If Mr. Elder didn't actually live here, where did he live? That had to be part of the answer.

She started to close the drawer when a shining bit of cloth caught her eye. It was folded between the ties. Gail pulled at it. It was a piece of yellow ribbon. Perk's yellow ribbon!

She heard a ringing in her ears and for a time she thought she was floating in space. Clutching the ribbon to her chest, she looked around the room. The naked women leered at her from their different poses. What had he done with Perk?

Feeling faint again, she pushed herself to her feet and clung to the dresser. Then she backed away, away from the dresser, the staring eyes of the naked women, backed to the door, reaching out, feeling for the doorknob. But she didn't find the knob. The door was open. She whirled around and came face to face with Mr. Elder.

He was frowning at her from under the ridge of his brow. His eyes went over her slowly, then settled on her hand, on the ribbon she held in it. He stepped into the room, his lips drawn back, exposing his rotten teeth. Then he reached out for her. His cold hand touched hers. Gail screamed. Hearing her own screams, remembering, reliving that time long ago, she threw back her head, opened her mouth wide, and screamed and screamed and screamed.

19

Imamu had listened to Gail's footsteps running down the stairs into the kitchen. He had walked into the living room and, breaking the unspoken rule of the Aimsley household, had sat in the stuffed chair sideways, swinging his feet. He looked at the painting. He had not been able to get it out of his mind. Now, thinking of what he had learned that day, he felt a closeness to it. What a strange land this neighborhood was—strange people. Yet the events he had heard about, all foreign to him, seemed somehow familiar.

Mrs. Briggs' tale had moved him almost to tears. Living in that big corner house, her soul crying for days—up and down that street, where little dreams, sprinkled on cold, hard concrete, were supposed to sprout into—more than trees. Don't leave me alone, lone, lone. All that loneliness. What about the loving, the caring? Old man Briggs had made

mistakes, but he sure had given a lot, or thought he
had. He had cared. So suppose he couldn't be con-
tained in a garden? Did that mean loving and caring didn't count?

What about his mother? Out there alone, a lone,
lone soul walking the streets. What was she looking
for in a bottle that was greater than his loving and
caring?

Where were the answers? Was he too young to
have them? Did anybody? Or was it so much a part
of life that there were no questions, no answers, just
facts—like with Mrs. Briggs?

Imamu pulled himself out of the chair and went
to stand in front of the painting. He studied the tiny
figures pushed together to create the depths of the
tormented sea. Before, the faces seemed mere dabs
of paint, carelessly applied. On closer scrutiny, he
could see that for those spinning around like match-
sticks in the whirlpool, with not even a toehold in
the sand, there was a sense of terror and of pleasure
on their faces at the same time—adding up to in-
tense relief at being sucked in, giving in to the forces
bent on crushing them into that mass.

Imamu felt the pull, the terror, the pleasure of
giving in. *Then he knew!* He was looking at the
results. Nevertheless, his feet ached to take off, his
body to be sucked in. He longed to feel the thrill of
just giving in! *He had found the intelligence of the
painting.* Yet he had to struggle . . . struggle . . .
struggle . . .

He heard Gail's footsteps on the stairs and pulled
himself away. Sweating, wild-eyed, burning from

his experience, he headed for the door. He was relieved that she had come, yet he did not want his feelings touched, or the hold of the picture on him broken. He had already run down the stoop when she called from the top of the stairway. "Imamu, what do you want for dinner?"

"Food," he called back and took off down the block.

But food was far from what he wanted. Too much was happening. The smell of the sea in his nostrils, the sound of the surf breaking against his ears, the roll of the waves around his head, the swirl, the undertow, the terror, the pleasure—but more—the knowledge. His body wanted more than food.

He walked quickly, the strange unearthly feeling building into jubilation. God, what a painting! And he had resisted it. And by resisting had joined it! Whatever anyone said, he knew he was no longer the ignorant sixteen-year-old street dude who had walked into the Aimsley household. He had reached another place. It had pushed him into a high. He felt the way dudes must feel after they had taken drugs. And just as a dude on a high needs that extra something, somebody, to share it with, he had to share his high with somebody.

His feet had been leading him in one direction. Dora Belle. He laughed, thinking of her. She owed him. She sure God owed him. She had promised. Titi, Titi, little Titi. He'd blow little Titi away. She didn't want that little man. She wanted him, Imamu. And she could have him. Alone, and willing. He rushed on, the heat in him like a strong wind, blowing him on.

"I take me bath and rub meself good, good, with sweet thing for me sweet man," she had told him once. Sweet man. Hot man. Impatient man—that was him. A man full of knowledge, as much man as a woman could want.

No more shucking and jiving, no more putting him on. Knowledge had made him free. She had to give now. And the word "no" had no meaning at all.

He ran up the stoop, opened the door, and stepped into her apartment, where the heavy smell of her perfume hit him. He listened for voices, the sound of another male. But only her heavy smell, strengthened by the moist heat of her shower, came through to him.

He heard her high-heeled slippers clicking from the bathroom to the bedroom. Good timing. He walked toward the bedroom. Hey, you want me, baby. You got me. Here I is. Sure, it was her need that had brought him. Her teasing, her double-meaning jokes, the heavy smell of her perfume, the sex she threw out of her black eyes. All that had brought him back, as she knew it had to.

He stood at her bedroom door, heard her humming, let the heady perfume drum in his head. And he knew that it did not matter what she wanted. He was here now. Her man. He pushed open the bedroom door and stood staring across the room at her.

Dora Belle sat at her dressing table, naked, her head bowed under the towel with which she was drying her hair. Imamu's eyes bulged at the sight of her firm flesh, the smooth stretch of brown skin that covered the full body. In the mirror, he saw her high breasts, her round stomach, and the pores of his body breathed. A sucking sound tickled his throat; it sounded loud enough to bring up Dora Belle's head. The towel fell down to her shoulders and they stared at each other in the mirror. Then the awareness of who they were, where they were, came through.

Dora Belle's black eyes grew bigger, and that was all Imamu saw for a while—her black eyes taking over her face. He wanted to run then, to slam the door, be long gone. He wanted to apologize, beg her forgiveness, but his throat closed. He wanted to close his mouth, too. But it hung open.

"What the ass you want in me house, you worthless son of a whore?" Her face twitched, her eyes narrowed, spit foamed at the corners of her mouth. "What you want in me house!"

"But . . . but . . ." He heard himself stutter, wanting to say the words he had thought to say when he had come. He wanted to explain the full reason he had decided to come. But words that were not of his choosing came sputtering out. "But Dora Belle," he heard himself say, "what happened to your hair?"

She was completely bald! Except for wispy strands of gray that had been raised by the brisk toweling, nothing was left of that long, soft, curling black hair, which had been a symbol of her pride, her beauty.

"You spying bitch!" she hissed, springing at him.

"I going fix your fronting ass! I going pave the road with your bowels so your foot will find it way."

Imamu's hands went out to hold her off, but he found her arms encircling his body. She wrestled him to the floor. On hands and knees, he scrambled to get away from her. She jumped onto his back, grabbed him by his neck. As he twisted in her powerful arms, fright added strength to his sixteen-year-old body, and using every muscle of his shoulders, his arms, he broke through her hold and crawled on his hands and knees to get out of the door. He scrambled to his feet, raced out of the house, and found himself on the street, running.

Blocks disappeared behind him; the sidewalks sank away. Imamu turned corners, more corners. He flew, flew away for his life. He had never been so scared.

Minutes later, out of breath, he stopped somewhere to lean against a lamppost, as air pumped back into his lungs in short painful gasps. He looked around—nothing was familiar. He was lost.

Darkness had settled thickly around, and not knowing the streets' twists and turns, he had ended up in a dead end. His feet moved, trying to walk back the way he had run, up one street, down another. When he finally stumbled on something familiar, it was Dora Belle's unfinished house near the corner of her block. He ran from the street in terror, turned more corners, raced blocks out of his way, trying to find his street.

By the time he found it, it was late. He knew that dinner had to be finished. Yet he hid himself a distance from the house, looking for Dora Belle's car, for signs of the woman herself, praying that she had not come after him. In the shadow of a tree, searching for her car under other trees, he tried to tell himself it was a joke. It was funny. He tried to laugh, at himself, at the funny sight he must have made running. From a woman? A plain woman? What did she get mad about, anyway? Hell, she wasn't the only somebody he knew who wore a wig. Lots of chicks wore wigs. Yet he knew that with Dora Belle it was different. And say what he wanted—he was scared.

"Anyway, her titties are for real." He tried to joke courage back into himself. "They sure ain't fooling around. No, sir. To think I lost out on that fine frame just be—"

Imamu's knees weakened. He doubled over as though from a blow to his solar plexus. He leaned against the tree for support. It was as though a mirror had been put before his mind. He knew suddenly and surely what had happened to Perk. He even knew where to find her.

20

Gail. What was she doing? He wanted her with him, needed her, her guts. She sure had them. But how to attract her without attracting everyone else? Imamu moved from the shadows toward the house, just as a neighbor's light went on, spotlighting him. He scuttled back under the tree. Why did he need a girl with him, anyway? She'd only say something silly—at the wrong time. Licking his parched lips, Imamu pushed Gail out of his mind and forced his reluctant feet to retrace their steps.

But this time he walked in the shadows, looking over his shoulder and dodging out of the way of approaching car lights. He was terrified; his heart pounded. But this was a different fear from the panic that had blown him out of Dora Belle's earlier. He was cool—doing what he had to do.

After he reached Dora Belle's street, Imamu stood across from her house, noticing with relief the low lights in her living room and her car parked outside. Was Peter Aimsley coming tonight? Maybe he ought to wait, make sure that everyone was in place before making a move. An excuse? Sure, he was scared. But waiting meant fear might take over.

A group of teen-aged boys walked by him. Not wanting to stand out alone, Imamu blended himself with them in a hop-stride saunter up the block, detaching himself when he arrived at Dora Belle's empty brownstone near the corner.

Imamu leaned against the stoop to look over the block. The darkness robbed folks of their identity. Voices sounded loud from different directions. But in the shadowed street, only flashes of white clothing stood out here and there. Imamu's white shirt made him feel like a target as he climbed the stoop of the vacant house and stood exposed, trying the door. It was locked.

He ran back down the steps and went to the side of the house. He pushed against the gate of the ground-level apartment. It was locked. He sauntered to the corner liquor store, where two groups of men, one going in, the other leaving, stood greeting each other, talking loud. Putting a toothpick in his mouth, Imamu tried to look relaxed as he waited for them to go their separate ways. At the same time he looked over the fence that divided the store from the house.

The fence ran alongside the house in an alley all the way back to the next street. Another fence joined it at a right angle behind the house, separating the backyards of the houses of the two streets.

The fence posed no problem—scaling fences had been a passion of his as long as he could remember. He slipped down the alley, and when he heard the see-you-soon promises of the men at the liquor store, he hoisted himself over.

He landed on his feet in the backyard of the brownstone. With a snarl a dog rushed him. Hot breath and a spurt of saliva hit his hand. Grabbing the fence again he pulled himself to the top, then realized that the dog was in the yard opposite. Trapped by the fence, the dog began to bark. Within seconds all the dogs in the neighborhood had joined in. Imamu let himself down and crouched in the shadows. He heard a door open, and for a nightmare of minutes, he waited. The dog's owner stood in the doorway, his shadow big in the shaft of light that reached out to Imamu.

A voice shouted, "Who out there? Anybody out there?" The dogs kept barking. After a few minutes the owner yelled, "Shut that noise up. If somebody was out there, wouldn't hear a sound from you." But he didn't come out to check. The door closed. The light went out.

Imamu waited, looking over Dora Belle's house. The back door was shut. Iron bars covered the windows off the garden. But above, on the first floor, the windows were partially opened. When the dog, having done its duty, stopped barking, Imamu walked up to the house and tried the door. It was locked, as he had supposed it would be. Fitting his sneakers between the bars of the ground floor window, he stood on the sill trying to reach

the ledge above. The tips of his fingers barely
touched. No sweat. He jumped down and found a
stone, which he put in his pocket, in case he needed
to break the window. Then he went back to the
barred window and fitted his feet between the bars
once again. A heave pushed his hand over the top.
His fingers caught, but only for a second; then he
lost his balance. The next try, he reached higher.
His fingers caught the ledge and held. Bringing up
his other hand he released his feet and swung free
for a second. He jammed his knees against the wall
and wriggled his body upward until he lodged a
forearm on the narrow ledge. He slipped his other
hand through the window and pushed it farther
open. It went up easily. First his shoulders, then
the rest of him twisted into the house.

The smell of paint was heavy in the room. On
hands and knees, Imamu crawled along the floor.
He bumped into what he supposed to be buckets
of paint and maneuvered around them, pushing
objects out of his way. He got to a doorway, stood
up, found and pushed the light switch on the wall.
The room was crowded with cans of paint and
turpentine, buckets, and paint brushes and rollers
left to dry on newspapers around the floor.

Moving quickly Imamu looked into the two large
closets in the room; they were empty. Switching off
the light, he left that room and walked through a
freshly painted hall to a front room. Lights from
the houses across the street shone directly into it,
and Imamu checked the closets. He went from room

to room on the first floor, searching them by the light coming in from across the street. All the rooms were empty.

In the dark he climbed upstairs. His feet crunched on fallen plaster; hanging cables threatened his face. At the top, he felt his way toward the back room and turned on the light. Having found it empty, he flicked off the light and moved to the front, where he repeated his search. In one of the rooms, near a window, he saw a figure. He went up and touched it: a bag of plaster of Paris.

Up to this time Imamu had not really allowed himself to think or feel, except for the tension created by the fear of being caught. His intention had been to search, find what he expected, and leave. But with the discovery of what he had thought to be a person, all his senses came alive. He was afraid now, not so much of being caught, but of being wrong.

Where would that leave him? Where would it leave him in relation to the Aimsleys? What about his sudden, sure intelligence? The imaginings of a kid? Naw. He shook his head. Things had changed. Somewhere, somehow things had been set up. This day had been spelled out. It had to be lived! And like his sudden understanding of the painting on Ann Aimsley's wall, the knowledge of what was happening had hit, and nothing would be again only what it had seemed.

On the top floor the light fixtures had been torn out of the walls. Imamu tripped on something and fell on his stomach, burying his face in a mound of dried plaster. As he scrambled to his knees, his hand touched something familiar: a flashlight. Sitting in the midst of the confusion, Imamu flashed it over the clutter of workmen's heavy picks, shovels, pails, slabs of walls rising in the center of the room.

It was impossible to find anyone in such confusion. Still he called: "Perk? Perky?" Tightening his stomach, he waited for an answer. He needed all his strength, because if she answered, he'd want to scuttle away like a rat. He didn't expect to find her alive.

He began to worry again. What if someone had seen the light? What if they called the police? They'd haul him in. And there was no telling them the truth of why he was here. They'd take him, keep him, and beg Dora Belle to press charges— and she would. All because he had caught her with her hair down. Imamu laughed in his throat.

And what if he found Perk? They'd haul him in quicker. Sullivan and Brown: "So that's where you hid her, hey, man? That's what we figgered. . . ." The story of a street boy's life.

Grimly, Imamu went down to the ground-floor apartment. He beamed the flashlight around. Nothing. But on the steps leading to the cellar, he paused. A feeling of danger came up to meet him, blocking his way. He stood, his fear growing, overwhelming him. What if Perk was down there? What if the police . . . He pushed his fears away, switched on the light on the stair wall, and went down, slowly. He remembered that the windows were painted black and the light would not be seen from the street.

The brightness of the cellar dazzled him. It was empty except for the new oil burner with its criss-crossing pipes, proud and showy. Imamu felt in his pocket for a toothpick, trying to hold back his disappointment. He had been so sure. The empty room mocked him. Where else? What else? Admit failure? He had laid everything—his experience, his knowledge, his street thing, his instincts—on this search. Everything that had been sharpened by his short and insightful suspension between two worlds had been into this, and everything had failed.

He turned to leave, to go back up the stairs. But as he took a step, then two, his heart thumped against his chest. A page turned over in his mind: What was the cellar doing so clean? When had the workers cleaned the basement? Why? They had left such a mess upstairs.

Imamu backed down and walked around the empty room. He tested the walls, inching his feet across the concrete floor. Then he saw it: A patch of concrete, about four feet square, newly laid and camouflaged with dirt to make it look as old as the rest of the floor.

Imamu's mind leaped. Get the hell out, it said. If you know what's good for you, if you value your freedom, then make it, baby, make it out of here.

But in his mind he had already climbed the steps, already chosen the pick and shovel he had to use.

Flashlight in hand, Imamu raced back to the top floor, swung the pick and shovel onto his shoulder, and went back to the cellar. Too much time had passed. It seemed to Imamu that the whole night had been spent searching. His street thing kept clanging—the odds against a dude's staying lucky for hours were high.

He lifted the pick and brought it down full force on the concrete square. The impact caused his bottom teeth to hit hard against his top teeth. A million lights swirled around before his eyes. Sixteen was not old enough for the kind of strength he needed.

Then at the same time something more vital, an almost-remembered something gave off another message. Smelling a strong, familiar perfume, he half turned and put out his hand, but the floor came rushing up to meet him, crashing into him.

21

Gail's screams hit the walls of the little room and bounced back against her ears. She moved away from Mr. Elder's reaching hand, knowing it was stupid to back into the room instead of trying for the door. But Mr. Elder kept moving forward, forcing her to go even farther into the room. The strange look on his face, his lips skinned back over brown, rotten teeth, held her fascinated.

"You come to see me?" He spoke softly. "But you ain't come when I here. I here now."

He kept advancing into the little room, forcing her to back away. And then her legs hit the bed. He reached out. Gail clutched the yellow ribbon desperately to her chest. She shifted, trying to get away from the bed, move around him. But he stood solidly in front of her, barring her way. His hand stayed outstretched, his strange smile mocking her.

But when his hand touched hers and she felt its cold lifelessness, Gail threw her head back in panic and screamed again, and again.

Mr. Elder drew away, the ridge of his overhanging brow pleating in anger. His thin body shook, and he smiled again as he moved to touch her.

Gail lowered her head and rammed it against his chest. Feeling his body fold, she raced past him out of the room, ran the length of the hall, down the stairs, past her floor, down to the first floor—where she collided with her mother, who was coming in from the store.

Ann Aimsley's groceries scattered over the foyer. "Gail, my God, what is the matter?"

"Mr. Elder . . . Mr. Elder . . ." Gail pushed her long, lean body into her mother's arms, snuggling into her.

"Mr. Elder?" Ann Aimsley asked. Then she directed her next question over Gail's head. "Mr. Elder, what has happened?"

Gail looked around to see the tall man coming down the stairs. "Don't let him touch me, Mother," she cried.

"What have you done to my child?" Ann Aimsley pushed Gail behind her and stood between her and Mr. Elder.

"Do to she?" Mr. Elder was indignant. "Ask she what she do to me . . . in me own room?"

"In your room!"

"Yes. In me room."

"Gail, what were you doing in Mr. Elder's room?"

"And that ain't the worse." Mr. Elder's voice was shaking. "She attack me. Me! Ann, you know I ain't a well man . . ."

"Attacked you? Gail . . ."

Gail clutched the yellow ribbon in her hand, feeling her mother's smallness, their vulnerability. And as though he had sensed her fear, Peter Aimsley walked through the open door behind them.

"Well," he said, looking at the three of them, the groceries all over the floor. "Damn, I got me a committee."

"I'm so glad you're home, Peter." His wife turned to him. "I don't understand what is happening."

"Daddy." Gail pushed herself into the shelter of her father's more capable arms.

"What's happening to my little girl?" he asked.

"Look." Gail thrust the yellow ribbon into her father's hand. "Look what I found in Mr. Elder's room."

"Mr. Elder's room?"

"In his drawer."

"In his drawer! What the hell you doing in Mr. Elder's drawers?"

"That's Perk's ribbon! Can't you see?" Gail screeched.

"Oh, my God!" Ann Aimsley stared at the ribbon. "Oh, my God . . ."

Peter Aimsley's eyebrows came together. "That my daughter's ribbon, man?" A silence quivered between the two men. Peter Aimsley repeated. "Man, whatcha doing with my lil girl's ribbon?"

The whites of Mr. Elder's eyes glistened. "What the hell you want to say?" he asked.

"Am asking man. I want to know. Whatcha doing with my lil girl's ribbon?"

"Your girl?" Mr. Elder's head pushed up out of his black coat. "And she ain't my girl, too? I ain't right in this house the day she born? I ain't watch she grow—the one sweetness in the house, in me life?" His eyes went from Peter Aimsley to his wife. "I ask you that. Now I want to ask, ain't I got right to one piece a she ribbon—when Ann sheself done give me?"

"I?" Ann Aimsley's eyebrows went up. "I?"

"You!" The main pointed a bony finger. "You give me—some birthday or the other. At a party, right here, in this house. She drop it and I ask you if I can keep it. And is you what tell me yes."

Puzzled, Ann Aimsley took the ribbon, looked at it, kept thinking about it. It was a ribbon like so many of Perk's, almost identical to the ribbon found in Imamu's room. But then Perk's favorite color was yellow. Finally Ann Aimsley spoke.

"It seems that I do remember something like that. But that was long ago—Perk's fifth birthday. That was the last party she had—"

"Is me ribbon." Mr. Elder held out his hand. "And I want it." Ann Aimsley held it away from him.

"Give it to him," Peter Aimsley ordered. She handed it to Mr. Elder, who took the ribbon and went haughtily up the steps. "Hey, man," Peter Aimsley called after him. "Man, I'm sorry. I just come in from work and . . ."

Mr. Elder stopped on the steps and looked down at his old friend. "You sorry! And me? Peter, it ain't in me heart to tell all you, but I telling just the same. It something wicked in the house." He pointed to Gail. "She! I never did see such a thing in me life—the way she treat me. Oh, she sweet mouth and pretty—on the outside. And I does hear people talk what a nice child and such. But when I see she on the street, she turn she head. In this house self, she rude, rude. She call me ugly. I does hear she. She ain't like people what ugly. But I the same me what did take she on me shoulder when she small—when I did look good. But I get the fever and change me look. Now, I so ugly it blind she brain—so she can't see good a-tall. It make she ugly! And I tell you, Peter, pain from the blind is pain, all the same." He walked up the stairs, leaving them. And neither Ann Aimsley nor her husband opened their mouths to protest.

To hear herself described in such a way jolted Gail. She searched deep in herself for the truth of his words. It wasn't so. She had always been good, had never done harm to anyone. "Daddy," she said, "he was with Perk—he left the house with her mornings . . ."

Her father turned away from her. "Ann, I'm hungry. What we got to eat?"

"Mother . . ." Gail said.

Ann Aimsley stooped to pick up her groceries. "Nothing yet," she answered her husband. "But is there anything wrong with franks and beans on the same table with steak and salad?"

"Not a damn thing," Peter Aimsley said, going up the stairs. "Long as it's on the table when I get down."

During dinner her parents kept looking away from her. Gail felt lonelier than she had ever felt in her life. She longed for Imamu. Whatever he thought about her—and he did disagree with her about Mr. Elder—he would take her seriously where it concerned Perk.

Gail looked at her mother. Had she really given him that ribbon? Three years ago! Ann Aimsley's eyes veered away from hers. So, she agreed with Mr. Elder that she was wicked? Ugly? Gail picked at the beans. She had wanted to talk about Mr. Elder's room, about the pictures on the walls. That would prove he had ideas . . . Didn't they want to know what happened to Perk?

"Where did you say Imamu went?" Ann Aimsley asked her. Gail swallowed. Words refused to come.

"Wherever he went," her father answered, "he'd better hurry back before I eat the rest of his steak."

"There's another piece I can cook for him," Ann Aimsley said. "I don't suppose hot dogs and beans will do anything for his appetite."

"Growing stud," Peter Aimsley said. "If a young

stud wants to put in time getting experience, he needs the kind of food to put hairs on his chest."

God! They were willing to talk about anything except Perk!

"From that I judge you think he went to Dora Belle's?" her mother asked.

"Where else?" Peter Aimsley shrugged.

"God, that's crude!" Gail burst out. "What makes..."

"I'm a crude man, baby," her father hit back at her. "Damn crude! It's my crudeness that put bread on this table. All them airs you put on. Making me accuse my best friend! That man helped me! He might even be responsible for us being here, in this house. Hell, he got me straight when I was young and wild—a perfect ass. And you got me accusing him! Where you get that stuff?"

Gail stared at her father. She had never heard such bitterness from him. Mr. Elder had turned him against her.

"You don't care anything about me," she cried. "You only take up for your friends! He tried to attack me when I was little but you didn't care! I screamed and cried and told you but you never cared. He could have done anything he wanted with me! Nobody cared..."

"Gail, Gail," Ann Aimsley said. "Don't say such things! The way you screamed and cried when Mr. Elder tried to kiss you when he came home from the hospital was because he had changed so much.

You had loved him before he went in. When he came back you didn't recognize him. Don't ever dare say he attacked you."

"Look," Peter Aimsley said, pushing back his chair. "Let's get out of here. Let's go on over to Dora Belle's. Ann, you owe her a visit anyway. And being away from this damn house might do us all some good."

22

But Dora Belle appeared unhappy at their visit. "Oh, is you?" she said to Peter Aimsley when she saw him at the door. "I ain't feel like company today a-tall."

Then looking behind him and seeing Gail and Ann Aimsley, she shrugged helplessly. "So the whole family come? And on me worse day. Well, if you must, come in then."

"You know I was coming for my taste," Peter Aimsley said. "Or did you let that Titi finish the rum up?"

"You know where it is better than me," Dora Belle said ungraciously and went to sit in the wing-backed chair and stared coldly at them from across the room. Ignoring her unfriendliness, Peter Aimsley went to the cabinet to get the rum.

"Something's happened." Ann Aimsley studied her friend from her seat on the couch. "I can always tell when someone's done something to Dora Belle. Who was it this time? Can I help?"

"But look at you, nuh?" Dora Belle snapped angrily. "Always helping, helping. Ann, ain't you tired a wiping people ass and getting no thanks a-tall?"

Gail stared at her godmother. Her words had an unsettling effect: Those good deeds, those noble gestures, they needed more than thanks—an altar really. But then, who was she to criticize? He had called her wicked. But she wasn't. Ugly, yes. But never wicked! God, the pain of being wrong, so wrong, for so many years! Why had no one told her? No one! Gail sulked as she sat looking at the two friends. She had looked at them without seeing them ever since her life began. She had thought she knew everything about them—but she didn't.

Her mother was jealous—for how long? How much did all that smiling and talking and sharing of children cover? And why? What a day of surprises—all this peeling back the cover of time, searching beneath life-styles and finding lifetimes of deceptions. Mrs. Briggs, her mother, even herself . . . What deep secret did Dora Belle's life-style cover?

"Dora Belle, what in the world is wrong? Tell me." Ann Aimsley pleaded. She cared. She was jealous and yet she cared.

"Oh, Dora Belle is still having trouble over that damn house." Peter Aimsley came back with two glasses of rum. "What happened? Those men aren't ready to start work?" He handed his wife a glass, then called: "Titi, Titi, bring the ice, man. What happened to that joker? Don't tell me he flew the coop."

"I tell you, I ain't want company." Dora Belle lashed out furiously. "And I ain't ready to make joke, either. What? You think it easy? People want to work? Ask a man to come make good money is like blasting a hole in the furnace a hell."

Gail saw that her father had handed Dora Belle a situation that she had seized on to justify her anger. Had they been using each other in this way all along?

"That's too bad, Dora Belle," Ann Aimsley said. "Mr. Miller knows some good contractors. Why don't I ask . . ."

"Where is Imamu?" Gail broke in to stop the small talk. Dora Belle had known Mr. Miller for years and had never asked him for workers and she wouldn't now.

"Oh? He ain't home?" Dora Belle asked.

"No, we thought he might be here," Ann Aimsley answered. "He didn't come for dinner."

"So you ain't see he tonight a-tall?" Then she relaxed. Easing down in the chair, she smiled suddenly at Gail. "Gail, honey, why you ain't go bring some ice for your mother?"

"He went out. He and Gail seem to think that by some magic he can find Perk, where the police have failed."

Gail sat for a moment, listening. She would get up and go to the kitchen and bring back ice, whether she wanted to or not, because that had to be her role. She had to be polite. They would all look at her and smile and be grateful when she came back. And the conversation would go on and on, never rising above the surface. She wanted to say no, she didn't want to get ice. But why? No reason. She didn't mind going. As a matter of fact, she would rather go than sit and listen.

Gail got up and left the living room. As she was passing through the foyer the door bell rang, and she turned to answer it. But Dora Belle got there first and opened the door.

"What you want, Titi?" Gail heard her say. "Ain't I tell you not to come trouble me today?"

"I just come to tell you that somebody is in your new house."

"You ain't say."

"Looks like it. I was looking out my window when I seen this light, see. Only for a second. But then it goes on on the next floor. And when I come out just now, I swear I seen a light go on in the cellar."

"How the cellar? Ain't the window paint black?"

"Yeah, but I was looking when the light came on. The black got bright, you know?"

"Okay, okay, is all right." She stopped him from going on. "It ain't nothing. I going just now . . ."

After closing the door, she went back to the living room and sat down. A second later she jumped up. "Look, all you know where things is. I coming now." She hurried out.

"Dora Belle is more upset than usual," Ann Aimsley said. "What do you think . . ."

"Probably one of her men," Peter Aimsley said. "I wouldn't be surprised if she let that young boy mess in her head."

"Daddy." Gail came into the room and interrupted him. "Someone's broken into Dora Belle's house. Aren't you going to help her?"

"Who said?"

"That little man who just rang the bell."

"But why didn't he call the police?" Ann Aimsley asked.

"You call them," Peter Aimsley said on his way to the door. Gail followed him, running behind him as he ran to catch Dora Belle.

But Dora Belle had disappeared into the darkness. And when they did see her, it was only briefly, under the street light, as she started to go into the new house. By the time they arrived, she had gone in and closed the door behind her.

Peter Aimsley ran up the steps and tried the door. It was locked. He rang the bell. It didn't work. He pounded on the door, but the heavy wood muffled his pounding. "That is a simple-assed thing to do," he muttered. "Locking a door when you go after burglars."

Leaning over the side of the stoop he tried the window. Locked.

"Light's still on in the cellar," Titi called up to him from the sidewalk.

"Man, why you ain't go in with her?" Peter Aimsley called back.

"She ain't ast me," the little man answered. "If she had wanted me, she'd ast me. But I bet it's one

a them mens. You know Dora Belle ain't had no
business locking them mens out and leaving all
they tools and things in there. Bound to be trouble.
Don't know why they ain't come before. Them some
big mens," he added.

"You think that's who's down there?"

The little man shrugged. "Who else? Ain't nothing in there but some cement and old pipes—and
them tools."

The house loomed over them, silent, the windows
darker than the night. For Gail, the dark silence
was disturbing. Why hadn't Dora Belle put on a
light? Why was no sound coming from that dark
interior? Dora Belle's weapon was her mouth. And
when it came to her houses, right or wrong, she
was a terror. Gail wanted to turn and run. Had her
mother called the police?

Her father had come down the stoop to get a rock
from the dead garden; going back up the steps, he
threw it against the window. The sound of shattering glass broke the deep silence around the house.
It also brought people from around the block.
They gathered in front of the stoop and watched
Peter Aimsley climb into the house.

Seconds later he opened the door, wide. No one
made a move to follow him inside except Gail. She
went into the house and bumped into her father in
the dark. "Why didn't that fool woman turn on
something?" he growled. "What she think, she a
cat or something?" The switch near the door didn't
work, nor did the switch in the foyer. They moved

together into the empty darkness. "That simple Titi," Peter Aimsley said. "Ain't nobody down there. I bet Dora Belle just forgot to turn off that light."

"Maybe," Gail whispered. But she did not agree. It seemed to her that she heard vibrations in the silence, as of loud thinking. She felt fear, terror, rising. "Why is she so quiet? What is she doing?"

Fumbling through the dark, using their knowledge of brownstones, they reached the stairs leading down to the ground-floor apartment, and touching the sides of the wall for balance, descended, gingerly. Then, shuffling though the darkness, they made their way to the cellar door, opened it, and found a swath of light brightening their way.

Gail caught her father's arm, checking his sudden move to run forward. She put her fingers against his mouth, and like conspirators, they tiptoed down the flight of stairs. Blinded by the brightness of the cellar, Gail shielded her eyes. Then, as she grew accustomed to the light, her intelligence refused to accept the bizarre scene being played out. Her first tendency was to laugh. But in that second Dora Belle had brought down a length of pipe on the head of the tall, thin man who was bending over, half facing her. Gail shouted when she saw him pitch forward.

"Imamu!" she cried out even before she recognized him. She rushed to kneel beside him. Peter Aimsley grabbed the pipe in Dora Belle's hand.

They wrestled. Madness streaked Dora Belle's face; saliva foamed at her mouth. Her fury made her Peter Aimsley's equal in strength. She tore the pipe away from him, then pushed him so hard he stepped back, stumbled over Imamu and Gail, and fell backwards. Dora Belle advanced on the three of them, the pipe raised in her hand.

High-pitched screams shattered the silence in the cellar. The screams tore though Gail, increasing her terror. But they also froze movement, and with it Dora Belle's uplifted arm. Peter Aimsley scrambled to his feet and jumped at Dora Belle, wresting the pipe from her hands. The screaming kept on. Gail turned to see her mother at the foot of the stairs, her mouth open, and in a strangely detached way, she said to herself: "Mother's hysterical."

"For God's sake, Dora Belle," Peter Aimsley shouted over his wife's screams. "It's me here. It's me!"

And as the screaming kept up, Gail hissed, "Mother!" and felt irrationally proud when the screams subsided.

Sanity struggled back to Dora Belle's face. Her bosom heaved. "Some thief break in," she gasped finally. "I come and find he."

"Imamu?" Ann Aimsley asked, her eyes searching out Gail's.

"Oh, is he? I ain't know is he," Dora Belle said in confusion. "I come and find he searching. I take something to he head . . ."

"Searching where?" Peter Aimsley said, looking

around the empty cellar. "What would the boy want to steal in this empty house?"

"Good as I be to he, too," Dora Belle said. "But you know how these boys is, Peter. They does thief anything. Pipe, faucet, whatever they does put they hand on. Is the drugs they does take."

"But Imamu doesn't take drugs," Ann Aimsley said.

"That's all you know, Ann dear." Dora Belle's tone was suggestive.

"But I know he doesn't." Gail challenged her.

"As for you . . ." Her godmother pointed her eyes at Gail, trying to silence her.

But it was Peter Aimsley who insisted; "Look, Imamu had a hell of a lot more over where you live. And I know you were pulling for him—"

"That how I mean," Dora Belle said. "Yet he come here . . ."

Imamu's eyes opened, and Gail called, "Imamu, Imamu." She tried to push him to a sitting position and noticed the hand she had put under his head was covered with blood. Helplessly, she called "Mother . . ." Ann Aimsley came to her and together they helped Imamu to his feet. Dazed, he looked around.

"He's hurt, Peter," Ann Aimsley said.

"Well, let's get him out of here and to a hospital," Peter Aimsley answered, going to support Imamu, who fell against him helplessly.

"Hospital," Dora Belle cried. "What hospital? The police. You put he in. You should a let he stay and dead. Why you get he out?"

"Come on," Ann Aimsley said, shocked by the vindictiveness in her friend's voice. "Let's hurry. The police will be here. I called . . ."

But Imamu struggled against them. He shook his head, then held it. "No, no, we can't go." His voice was blurred. "Gail . . . Gail . . . she's here. Perk . . ."

"What you say, boy?" Peter Aimsley asked, gruffly, not hearing. But Gail had heard. And for the first time she looked around the cellar, noticed the spot where Imamu had fallen, the newness of the concrete, the pick.

Dora Belle's eyes had followed hers, and now she said, "Come, let we get he out." She started to the door, leading them. But Gail kept asking Imamu:

"Imamu, what do you mean? Tell me. What is it?"

"Perk." He spoke weakly. "Perk."

"What's he mumbling about?" Peter Aimsley shouted.

"Perk's here, Daddy. Perk is there!" Gail pointed to the new spot under the fallen pick.

"What foolishness," Peter Aimsley growled. "Look, let's get this kid to the hospital. He's losing his mind."

"Can't you see?" Gail cried in desperation. "That's what Imamu was doing here. That's the only reason he'd be here. We were looking . . ."

Supporting Imamu under the arms, Peter Aimsley turned to go. But then he looked at his wife. She was staring at Dora Belle in such terror that he could not ignore it. Letting go of Imamu's inert frame, he rushed back, picked up the ax, and dug down into the concrete. Once, twice, the concrete cracked.

The rest of them stood watching, fascinated. Gail moved over to Imamu, held him, kept holding on to him, hoping it was not so. Praying he was wrong, wishing that the concrete would not give, but knowing that it had to be done—and later put behind them, right or wrong.

They were still watching the cracks grow in the concrete when, minutes later, they heard heavy footsteps pounding down the steps. Two uniformed policemen entered the cellar. Ann Aimsley moved to stand near her husband. Gail held on to Imamu, supporting him, belligerently protecting him.

Dora Belle broke into a shrill accusation: "Is he. Is he," she cried, pointing to Imamu. "If you does find anything, he the one what do it. He the one what put she there. You see so, Ann? Peter? How he know she there if he ain't put she?"

"What's going on?" one of the policemen asked.

"My sister's buried there." Gail spoke positively. She pointed to the spot where her father was digging.

The policemen elbowed Peter Aimsley aside, one grabbing the pick from him, the other picking up the shovel. They kept on where he had left off, cracking the concrete, then removing the cracked pieces with the shovel until they were digging through dirt.

Gail hugged Imamu, not wanting to see. She had believed him, when her parents might have doubted him. But the moment Peter Aimsley had grabbed that shovel, he had been sure of what he would find. Her mother knew. Their feelings had been transmitted to her without words, through whatever made them a family. But now she wanted Imamu to be wrong. She wanted them to be wrong. She wished this part of the night to be a dream, she wanted to awaken on their quiet street, sitting on the stoop discussing probabilities. She wanted to find Perk, but sometime in the future, where there was no ground to dig, but only a hint, a clue that they were going to find her alive.

"Oh, God. Oh, my God, my God, my God." Her mother's anguish withered all her hopes. Imamu had gained strength, and now it was he who was holding her, holding her to him, trying to stop her from looking. But she had to see, had to see her mother, try to spare her mother, her father, who were as dear to her as her life.

At first she saw only the little hand—the fist, decomposed, but stretching up out of the shallow grave. And then it relaxed, opened, releasing a treasure it had been holding: a chain, a locket, a gold locket. And once the treasure was released, the hand collapsed.

Peter Aimsley grabbed his wife, pulling her to him, pressing her face into his chest as though by shielding her from the sight, he could obliterate it. He held her, pulled into him, merging their suffering. But the shrill suffering scream tearing through the small basement, separated each one, forced each one to take a measure of his own suffering.

Dora Belle, her face twisted, shrieked, twisting

their insides: "Oh, God, oh, God, is she! Is she! Yes. Take she. Give she a decent burial. I ain't want she to lie there day in and day out in me mind, in me heart, on me soul. Ann, I ain't mean it! The little thing come to me house early, early. I ain't yet dress. I hear she calling, 'Godmother, I want you to comb me hair. We got a party.' Before I get up to lock me bedroom, she run in. She stand there looking. Just so. Looking. 'Godmother,' she say, 'but you ain't got no hair. You ain't got no hair a-tall.'

"I grab she to shake she. I let she go. She fall and hit she head on me bureau. I pick she up. She done dead. But I ain't mean it. Ann, Peter. You know I did love she. Oh, God, I did love she. She was me heart . . ."

23

"It just had to be, that's all." Imamu wished he could sit sideways so that he could look at the painting while he talked, without having to turn his head. Mrs. Aimsley had taken the plastic covers off the furniture for the funeral and had kept them off all week. But it was still impossible to relax enough to sit sideways when the custom had been so formal—at least not while she was looking at him.

"You know how it is, Gail? It's like I been telling you. It's being out there," he said. And as he spoke, he noticed how the morning sun caught a bit of yellow in the whiteness of the surf.

Gail looked at him. She was pouting. "You keep telling me, Imamu, but I don't get the connection. I guess I need you to draw pictures."

Imamu gazed at the painting. Maybe he didn't understand either. Maybe his stumbling in on Dora Belle and the pieces' falling together had been an accident. He didn't think so. All along, things had been adding up. When the answer came, it just made sense.

Sure, it stood to reason that being out there had given him advantages. But they'd never see that. They were programmed to suffer the pain of his being disadvantaged for their own benefit.

In a way, that's what had given him the clue—the painting.

Sitting naked in that precinct while Brown and Sullivan did him, he had dug that his punishment had nothing to do with Perk. What had happened then had been happening to him long before he had even seen Brooklyn. Just like his fellow sufferer, the dude who had taken six years to do that painting. Then he had lost his pad, and that had had nothing to do with what he was about. So it stood to reason that what was happening, what had happened to Perk, had started long before he showed on the scene.

Imamu lowered his eyes to the Aimsleys, sitting on the couch beneath the painting. Peter Aimsley had carried that stunned look all week. He looked wasted—a man down for a long count with his grief. Ann Aimsley, though, looked good. Sure, she had a look of suffering in her brown eyes, but the two-piece suit she was wearing with the blouse frilled at the neck made her look her old efficient self. There was something else . . .

"You really love that painting, don't you, Imamu?" she said when she caught his eye.

"Yes, ma'am."

"Then it's yours. That is"—she looked from Gail to her husband—"if neither of you object." They both stared at her. "Don't look so shocked," she cried. "It's just that—well, with Perk gone—and Dora Belle—that business of just needing to—"

"To be perfect?" Imamu said. He wanted to add, there's no need to prove anything, no need for reminders of mistakes.

"I don't know . . ." she said.

But Imamu knew. Now the plastic covers were gone, and the furniture could be worn into a graceful old age— And that was it! The ropelike veins on Ann Aimsley's neck had disappeared. The tension on her face was gone. She looked at ease with herself. God, it had to be hell, living in the shade of all that beauty. How many years!

He sat up. But instead of speaking about his insight, he decided to bind her to her words, ruthlessly. "Thanks," he said. Then, wanting others to bear witness, he added, "Sure is good of you, Mrs. Aimsley. Gail, ain't that boss of your mother? Imagine giving me that painting!"

Gail, too, had been studying her mother. "You still didn't tell me what led you to that particular cellar, Imamu," she said.

"I did. You just ain't been listening."

"Tell me again."

"Well, I went over with my cut hand, see? Dora Belle was coming out of that house, right? She was— Well she was looking bad—for Dora Belle. You know she don't go out on the street looking bad. Don't get me wrong. Even when she looked

bad, she looked good to me. Dora Belle is fabulous."
He looked up quickly to make sure he hadn't
offended Ann Aimsley. But she had that well in
hand. "Well, she started loud talking about have
to do this and that—including taking bags of garbage out by herself.

"Now, you know and I know that Dora Belle
don't be doing no work on her own—not when she
got turkeys around ready to do whatever she wants.
So why the loud talk? Why the great scene? Next
she takes me in hand—does herself up—and I ain't
seen Dora Belle looking tacky again. Dig? You
ever seen her look bad?"

"Sometimes she looks better than others," Gail
answered.

"But I mean bad?"

"No."

"Ri-ight. Then, too, why did the workers cut out?
I know Dora Belle is sharp with the tongue—but
there was one joker, the day before, who was looking at her like he'd work for nothing. All she had
to do was stop being nasty and ask." Imamu stuck
a toothpick in his mouth. "And so a piece here and
a piece there . . . know what I mean?"

"I'm listening," she said with a sigh.

Imamu took the toothpick out of his mouth, then
put it back again. It was too hard to explain. He
didn't have the words. He never had had words.
How could he explain Mrs. Briggs, and the painting—the whole thing? "It's all around you." He
threw out his arms to include the entire room.

"If you saw so much, why didn't you say something?" Gail asked. "To think that I accused Mr. Elder—"

"But that's all a part of it," Imamu cried.

"Part of what?"

"I don't know." Imamu gave up. "I guess it only got to do with the way I look at folks."

That was true. Living in this house had been like looking from outside through a window into a place where he knew he had been before. The setting was different. All fixed up to hide things.

Imamu stood up, stretched, and walked to the window. A street looking so good ought to be different. Only pretty things ought to happen on such a street. But the same things happened here as out there. But out there, there were no trees to hide things. Everything out there was raw, bare-assed.

Gail, so pretty, sharp-thinking, intelligent, innocent—because of the trees? That was it! Innocence had robbed her of being truly beautiful. That innocence that her parents were proud of, that the neighbors admired, that innocence had got her all twisted. Twisting things into right-wrong, pretty-ugly, good-bad. Damn. The world was too real to afford her all that innocence. Somebody had to pay. Perk?

Staring out at the quiet street, Imamu heard the wind move the branches so that branch knocked against branch. The sun shone, yet the trees held their shadows. That moved him, made him understand—in a way—how much somebody like Gail had to dig through in order to see. One thing she had going for her though: courage.

"What an unhappy time." Imamu turned as Mr. Elder came into the living room. "I just come back from seeing Dora Belle," he said. "She ain't want to see me. The woman mad. But who else? I all she got."

"Do you think that she will plead insanity?" Ann Aimsley asked.

Mr. Elder shook his head. "She mad, true. Mad with pride—a deadly sin." He looked around the room, his unhappiness hanging around him like the black coat he wore. "So criminal. All the woman want is a man, you know? To love she. To care for she. But I—I too ugly. Lord, if only I did know how far she'd go."

"Mr. Elder." Imamu stopped him as he turned to leave. "You knew?"

"Yes, I did know."

"What!" Peter Aimsley lifted his head and looked at his old friend, disbelief bringing him to his feet. "You knew and didn't say nothing to me? Man—"

"No, Peter." Mr. Elder shook his head. "Not about that—"

"About what then?"

"That she lost her hair, man," Imamu answered. "Mr. Elder, what's with this sickness?"

"Peter know."

"You all got some kind of fever, right? You gave it to her—"

"Or she might have given it to him," Peter Aimsley answered. "Some kind of tropical fever, they didn't have no cure. Folks died from it. Dora Belle was kind of wild then. Sailors, merchant marines—

from all over the world. She had been going with Elder a long time then. Wanted to get married—"

"Whatever, the fever did me bad, bad. I lose me fat. I lose me flesh. I lose me teeth. She only lose she hair—and she gone mad. Oh, God," he cried unhappily, "what is this thing, vanity? I did know she break with Jacques on that account—or he break with she. You know them complexy people, they like good hair. That was hard for she to take—all that waste a she young years, then . . ." He stopped speaking and left them. Imamu went to the foyer to pick up his duffel.

"Guess I better cut now."

Gail came out after him. She went to the foot of the stairs and called, "Mr. Elder, I want to thank you for how much you helped us with the funeral. If it hadn't been for you and mother . . ."

The tall man looked down at her, cleared his throat with a loud *huurmph*, and kept on going.

"Mr. Elder," she called again. "I know I'm pretty old to be anybody's little girl . . . but I'm not too old to beg . . ."

The man turned, looked down at her again, looked hard, then nodded, bowed his head, and turned into the dark at the top of the stairs. Imamu smiled. She sure did have that courage working for her.

"Look, you got to come to see me," he said to her. "It's kind of rough up there. But you'll have me to look after you."

"What can keep me away?"

"Promise?"

"Promise."

Ann and Peter Aimsley came to the living room door. Imamu expected the man to break in—tell her the way the game was to be played. But he didn't.

"Is there anything I can say to change your mind?" Ann Aimsley asked.

"Naw, I got to go."

"If it's because of the way I been acting, man . . ." Peter Aimsley smiled his wistful little lost-boy smile.

Imamu shook his head. "The way I figger, I owe it to my old lady. The house look like a junkyard. Maybe if I did a little fixing, be there to make sure she looks after herself, she might get to wanting to pull herself together. Anyway, she needs me."

"What if she doesn't want you?" Gail asked.

"She does. She just don't know it. Anyway, I know it. And the way I see it, a dude got to keep moving from where he's at. Get what I mean?"

Of course she didn't. Folks like her just didn't see disadvantage as being a plus. They couldn't. But she tried. Deep in his eyes she tried. That gave him a way-out feeling in the pit of his stomach, a sadness that he had opted for pulling out instead of being with her. He dug her. He sure as hell dug her. "Anyway"—he passed his eyes over her from her head to her feet and then back again—"don't make sense us being together all the time. In the same house? We ain't no brother and sister. And we ain't about to be. Right?"

"Ri-ight," she said, blushing.

"What about your painting?" Ann Aimsley asked. "Aren't you taking it with you?"

"Naw, I ain't ready for it yet. Got to get the right kind of pad to hang it. Dig? I owe that dude. Until then, let it hang where it's at so we all can dig. You ain't losing me, you know. I'm just expanding— see where I'm coming from?"

Peter Aimsley grabbed Imamu's hand and shook it. "They mightn't understand where you coming from, man, but I hear you. You know I been *out there*. Tell you, when I was your age I started work- ing—in that shop, the same one. I own it today—"

"Yeah, yeah, I know." Imamu cut him off. He grabbed his duffel bag, hoisted it on to his shoulder. "But what say I drop around your shop for a look- see one day? I mean, when you ain't too busy."

"Busy! How you sound, clown? I ain't never too busy when you got time. Right?"

"Ri-ight."

Imamu adjusted his duffel and walked out of the door.

ABOUT THE AUTHOR

Rosa Guy was born in Trinidad and grew up in Harlem. Ms. Guy is the author of a recently completed trilogy about American and West Indian young women: *The Friends*, an ALA Notable Book, *Ruby*, and *Edith Jackson*, both selected as Best Books for Young Adults by the Young Adult Services Division of the American Library Association. Her work has been widely acclaimed for its skillful delineation of what Ms. Guy has called the grotesque in life and character.

A founder of the Harlem Writers Guild, Ms. Guy lives in New York City and is at work on a new novel.